Death After Evensong

Douglas Clark

© Douglas Clark 1969

Douglas Clark has asserted his rights under the Copyright, Design and Patents Act, 1988, to be identified as the author of this work.

First published in 1969 by Cassell & Company Ltd.

This edition published in 2018 by Endeavour Press Ltd.

For Patsy

Table of Contents

Chapter One	7
Chapter Two	25
Chapter Three	49
Chapter Four	70
Chapter Five	89
Chapter Six	105
Chapter Seven	123

Chapter One

Big Ben struck eleven. Detective Sergeant Brant finished stowing the four murder bags. He leaned against the force of the north-east gale as he went the few steps to the driving seat. His oppo, Detective Sergeant Hill, sitting in the passenger seat, shivered as the door opened. He said: 'For God's sake start her up and switch the heater on.' Brant did as he was told. He revved gently to get the warm air circulating and said: 'Where're we going?'

'Haven't a clue. But I do know my missus was upset when I phoned to tell her I'd likely be away for a day or two. If she hasn't got me in bed with her in weather like this her beef gets chilled.'

'And you get the cold shoulder! I know. But I'm more interested in how the Chief's pulse is beating than in your old woman's frozen limits.'

Hill was sergeant to Detective Chief Inspector George Masters. There was a lot of loyalty between them. He didn't want to say straight out that Masters had been making his life a little hell for weeks past. And in any case Brant knew it already. That's why he'd mentioned the Chief's blood pressure. So Hill said: 'His temper's not too bad. He's got a new suit on. That usually makes him feel better.'

'You should know.'

Masters and Detective Inspector Green came out of the new Yard building together, not talking. They never talked much. Not to each other. There was no love lost. They felt too uncomfortable in each other's presence to communicate either readily or unnecessarily. It was their misfortune—typical of the contrariness of life—always to be officially paired for murder enquiries. Green was cursing himself for not having put in the request for a transfer he'd been contemplating—and putting off—ever since he'd started to work with Masters. He was cursing Masters, too. For making him feel inferior and awkward. For being—in Green's opinion—one of those officers who do more than their fair share of creeping to fiddle promotion above older and better coppers—such as Green himself.

Masters towered above Green who, though well up to minimum height requirements, looked dumpy and squat beside him. Masters was thinking about Green. Thinking it was time the Inspector quickened his step to get to the car first. He guessed Green thought nobody had noticed this habit of his. But Masters had rumbled that Green was nervous in traffic: had a phobia about getting chopped from behind by an overtaking vehicle if he sat in the offside seat. So he made sure he always got the nearside. With a mental surge of cynical pleasure at being proved right, Masters watched Green forge ahead. He thought Green a fool. Not for being afraid—Masters could well understand and have sympathy with that—but because he hadn't cottoned on that when Brant drove a police car nothing ever did overtake it.

Masters took off his Crombie coat. He folded and carefully built it into a symbolic barrier between himself and Green on the bench seat. He said to Brant: 'Take the A1 and make sure you're near a decent pub at one o'clock.' After that nobody said a word till they'd cleared Apex corner. Then, because the traffic was a little less frightening for him, Green asked: 'Can we know where we're going and what for? Or would that be telling?'

Masters waited just long enough to let Green think he wasn't going to get a reply and then said: 'The Soke Division has asked for help. They've had a parson murdered. The vicar of Rooksby-le-Soken.'

Surprisingly, Green said: 'Like Becket? In his own church?'

Masters thought Green sounded hopeful. Knew he would be. If anything, Green was a chapel-goer. He'd been brought up that way because his parents had once heard and ever thereafter believed that the established church was the Conservative Party at prayer. And the Greens were more than left inclined.

Masters said: 'In a schoolroom.'

Hill had a road map open on his knees. 'Where is this Rooksby something or other? I've never heard of it.'

'Neither had I until an hour ago. It's in the middle of a peat bog, miles from anywhere . . .'

'Got it. We've over a hundred miles to go. Just our luck to have to go north in February.' His words jerked a mutual response. As if by consent they all peered through the misty windows at the cold greyness outside. The wind moaned as it whipped past the speeding car. Green wiped a clear patch with his sleeve, and without looking at Masters, said: 'Anything else? Or is this a blind date?'

'Very little. He was killed before midnight and not found until eight this morning.'

'A bit quick in calling us in, weren't they?'

Masters said, trying to needle Green: 'P'raps they were frightened of the Establishment—the Established Church.'

He got his response. 'Why have a bishop biting your ear if you can offload on to somebody else? I'll bet they haven't got as much as one suspect.'

Masters said: 'No suspect, no weapon, and no motive. All they know is he was shot. Nothing more. And I'll bet that's the reason for calling us in straight away.'

'I can't see it's any excuse for dodging the job,' Green said grumpily. 'It should have been a challenge for them. No suspect? No idea is more like it! Real N.A.A.F.I. characters if you ask me.'

Hill acted as straight man. 'N.A.A.F.I. characters?'

'No aim, ambition, and flog-all initiative.' The petty triumph pleased Green. He turned to Masters. 'How many characters in this Rooksby dump?'

'According to the Gazetteer, just over two thousand.'

'I knew it. They couldn't find one suspect. We'll have two thousand, not counting the big wide world outside.'

Masters was getting bored with grumbles. He didn't answer. He'd told them all he knew. He took the pipe from his breast pocket where it was wedged upright by a white silk handkerchief and filled it from a new, brassy tin of Warlock Flake. Irritably he brushed a few scattered fragments of tobacco from the trousers of the new suit—a dark Keith and Henderson cloth his tailor had said would be kind to the figure. Not that Masters had to worry about his figure. He was as lithe and fit as any man in his early thirties: no belly or incipient paunch. But he was built so physically big that sheer bulk dictated care. He'd appreciated this when, reluctantly playing Santa Claus at a Police Children's Party, he found his great size frightening more than delighting the small guests.

Masters dressed well. As a bachelor he could afford to spend more money on clothes than his colleagues. And there was no doubt in his own mind—or that of anybody at the Yard—that he was vain. Not only about clothes, but about his successes and resultant reputation. Even about his fine, slim hands that seemed as though they should have belonged to a man of infinitely sensitive, slender build—a virtuoso pianist or precision craftsman. Masters consciously cultivated vanity. As a way of flying a personal flag among a group of conformists. But, contrary to Hill's earlier statement, he was not getting his usual pleasure from the slightly stiff, unworn feeling of the new suit. Masters was feeling peeved.

It was a sensation that had been building up for nearly four months. Ever since he'd insisted on charging Joan Parker with manslaughter instead of murder. He'd known she'd be found not guilty of murder, and he'd wanted a charge that would stick. Joan Parker had got three years, but because she was an above average good looker, the buzz was that Masters had protected her because he wanted her for himself. His colleagues appreciated this. But with a sexually invigorated understanding that manifested itself in mawkish pity. Pity because no policeman is allowed to have any form of relationship with a prisoner. And here—or so they thought—was Masters growing daily more bad-tempered from frustrated lust.

They were wrong. It was the pity that was peeving Masters. He resented being treated like an idiot child. And he suspected Green of originating the rumours. But they were right in thinking he wanted Joan Parker. Wanted her as he had wanted no other woman in his life. But they hadn't the mental penetration to see through the situation as it really was. He hadn't wanted to spare Joan Parker. Just the reverse. He'd wanted to make sure, without the slightest doubt, that she paid for killing a man. He believed in punishment for crime as passionately as he wanted Joan Parker. But he couldn't hammer his reasons home without baring his soul. Vanity wouldn't let him do it: and Green was the last man on earth to fathom motives like this unaided. An iron ring of misunderstanding was being forged. Masters grew peeved. It was taken as a sign that he really had forced the hand of justice to favour a girl he fancied a tumble with. This image hurt his vanity. He grew more peeved. Rancour swelled like a malignant growth clutching at his guts.

As the car headed into the screaming wind he sat silent and glowered. His attitude affected the others. Hill was thinking the atmosphere inside was as icy as outside. Brant drove with more than usual care, not daring to risk a single hairy moment with Masters in his present mood. Green was damning Joan Parker's eyes. He guessed she must be haunting Masters day and night. He could visualize her by day—in a cell. He wondered what she would look like by night—out of prison. His imagination was not up to it. Joan Parker was not like any woman he'd ever known. A hell of a figure!

So slim that he thought she would break in two if she tangled good and proper with a man the size of Masters.

*

Before three o'clock they were nearing Rooksby. Cutting across flat countryside unrelieved except where rows of windswept trees showed the courses of lodes, canals, dykes and drains. All running straight as arrows for miles. Sluggish, dull water, lapping a few inches below the tops of banks. Whipped by the wind into fan-shaped ripples. The earth as dark and heavy as treacle where it had been winter dug. Grass growing tuftily: red near the roots as grass on fitties always is. The dead remains of samphire and bobbly sea pinks standing up from smooth bare mud. A rare patch of early aconite or snowdrop showing up golden or livid in the gloom. Farm labourers' cottages clinging in lonely pairs, stark, unlovely and seemingly as lifeless as the bare trees planted as windbreaks.

Green said: 'This place would drive anybody to murder.'

Masters said nothing for a moment. Just as Green was beginning to think him an offensive big-head he said: 'German doctors are investigating the effects of weather on the human psyche. They've established that more people suffer coronaries in hot weather than cold. More people get headaches in close, oppressive weather . . .'

Green interrupted. 'I could have told them that. And how wind affects people. Look how the Wogs are driven mad by khamseens.'

Masters knocked his pipe out in the ashtray. 'Suggesting that Englishmen may be driven to murdering parsons by cold nor'easters?'

'Why not? They're depressing, aren't they?'

'Parsons?'

'Cold winds. And murderers are manic depressives—or some of them are.'

The car bumped over a level crossing outside a deserted station. The sign said it was Rooksby-le-Soken Halt. Apart from the station house and a few tumbledown coalsheds there was no sign of habitation. They came to the outskirts of the village three-quarters of a mile on. First a couple of dozen new council houses, characterless in immature gardens: monuments to poor taste and bad siting. The road jinked to avoid them. Brant cursed all planners. 'They couldn't have straightened out this death trap while they were at it, could they?'

Hill said: 'And look what they've built just round the corner!'

They went on slowly. Masters gazed across an asphalt playground at a new school. Through the boundary palings he saw single-storied, glass-walled classrooms strung out in great wings from a brick-built nucleus. Lights were burning, illuminating an end-on view of rows of children, listening to teachers, with their hands in the air, reading. He got the impression the kids were miserable. There seemed to be no vivacity in the fish tank. Probably the weather. And because it was nearly the end of a long day.

'If the parson was knocked off in one of those showcases it must have been a public performance,' Green said.

'The footlights would be off on Sunday night.'

There was a gap of two hundred yards before the start of the older part of Rooksby. Half-way along it, cornerwise on to the road, was a tall factory building. The brickwork had a whitish, dusty coating. The small, square windows showed dim, rounded patches of light as though snow had piled up inside the frames. Green said: 'It's a flour mill. The dust gets everywhere.'

As they went past, a second side came into view: the front elevation. The sign showed Green had been near the mark: Rooks by Instant Potato. Green said—probably for the first time in his life—'My mistake. Spud flour. My missus uses it for cottage pies.'

Hill said: 'Cottage? Or Shepherd's?'

'What's the difference?'

'One's got slices of spud on top. The other's got mash. I can never remember which.'

The road narrowed between old buildings. Only the pavement on their left survived. There was no room for the other. The Road Narrows and Extreme Care signs had to be on overhead arms sticking out from the walls. No space for posts. Masters said: 'Keep your eyes open for the station. It must be about here somewhere and it won't have room outside for as much as a blue lamp.'

So far they had passed no shops. There was just enough variety in the shape, size and age of the houses to give Rooksby its first hint of character. Then came near-disaster. A barrow—a modern seesaw of tubular alloy on pneumatic tyres—was the cause. The crossroads—a little lane hidden by high walls came in at right angles—was unexpected. So was the barrow. It shot out at a trot. A middle-aged man the motive power. Dressed in a shopkeeper's coat of pale brown drill. His scrubby hair peaked at the top and his ears stood out like red jug handles. His load was a pyramid of multi-coloured buckets and bowls in plastic. Brant swore. The force of his foot on the brake lifted him from his seat. There was the bray of a ratchet as Hill dragged on the handbrake. The Vauxhall responded humpily. Its bows dipped to a stop less than a foot from the barrow.

The man appeared to be unaffected. He backed his trolley and brought it and himself alongside Brant. He said: 'You want to watch it, mate.'

Brant, red and angry, said through his teeth: 'You crossed without warning. I'm on the main road. I've got the right of way.'

'Not in Rooksby you ain't. People that live here have the right of way—always. Not outners.'

Brant said: 'Careful. Or I'll have you for not being in proper control of that contraption.'

The man cackled with laughter. 'You'll what? You just try it, mate. Go on. Try it. You'll have another think coming.'

Brant glanced round at Masters for instructions. Masters growled: 'Drive on. And keep a look out for the police station.'

The man neighed even louder, and edged the corner of his trolley across Brant's offside front wheel. 'Police station? What police station?'

Green said: 'Are you trying to say there are no police in Rooksby?'

'Oh, aye. There's two on 'em. But they haven't got a police station. Only a front bedroom. And I wouldn't go there if you know what's good for you. They're too busy with parson's murder to do with outners. But if you do go, I'll go as well.'

'What for?'

'To say how you came speeding through here and nearly killed me.' He grinned in triumph. 'They'll believe me against all outners. They allus do. Speeding through here's the only cases they get to show they're earning their money.'

Masters growled angrily. What he said was drowned in the hissing of heavy brakes and a blast on a horn behind them. Green jumped in his seat. The shopkeeper cupped his hand and shouted, shrill above the pounding of the heavy engine, to the driver of the ten-tonner: 'Shan't keep you more'n a sec, Ted. These outners was speeding through and nearly killed me. Just warning them.' Ted was thick set and florid, and muffled against the cold. He leaned half out of his cab and roared: 'Get the perishers out of the way, Perce. Quick! I've got to get to Barrett's and back with a load before knocking off.'

Perce did as he was told. Hastily. He pulled his trolley clear and said derisively: 'Shove off! And don't come by here again in a hurry.' Ted honked behind. Masters grunted. Brant set the car in motion and Green said to Perce: 'I'll get you, loop lugs. See if I don't.'

The road widened out into a square. Brant pulled to the left. Ted accelerated past him to storm out of sight on the far side. Hill said: 'This is it.' Brant stopped level with a board where a notice warning about the dangers of the Colorado Beetle flapped in the wind. Masters got out and looked over the car roof at the two cement-rendered police houses. Semi-detached at the upper storey, with a broad tunnel between them at ground level. A face appeared momentarily at the window above the tunnel. A few seconds later a door half-way down the side of the tunnel opened and a plain-clothes man hurried out to them at a muscle-bound half-run. He introduced himself: 'Nicholson. Detective Superintendent.'

They trooped down the tunnel and up a flight of uncarpeted stairs with a rope balustrade. Nicholson said: 'This is the office. Part of both houses, but belonging to neither, if you see what I mean.'

Masters was impressed. He'd often worked from drab stations. This was more comfortable and lived-in than he had expected or hoped for. There was a bright fire with a bucket of coal and a heap of fuzzy peat blocks on the hearth: two easy chairs and the carver from an old dining set: on the table a red chenille cloth stained with ink blots and fringed with bobbles: on the floor a square of straw-coloured, broadloom Armadillo matting. In an alcove was a modern sink unit with a two-burner gas ring and a kettle on the draining board. Nicholson introduced a young constable: 'P.C. Crome. He was the one called to the body.' He turned to Masters. 'Crome's one of the two stationed here in Rooksby. The other is Senior Constable Vanden, who'll be seeing the kids across the road after school before reporting back for a cup of tea.' He raised his voice. 'And talking of tea, jump to it, Crome, lad. Our visitors'll want a pot of hot and strong, and I'm feeling dry myself.'

Masters was summing up Nicholson. The superintendent was heavily built and still fair-haired where a dark man might have turned grey. He put Masters in mind of a retired professional footballer. He moved with the forward slant and the stiff, hunched gait of a man who had done too much physical training earlier in life and was now taking no exercise at all.

The tea came up dark in blue and white banded mugs. Masters gulped a mouthful and said to Nicholson: 'You called us in a bit quick, didn't you?'

'I knew we'd have to have you as soon as I saw the body. Too fishy right from the word go. And when we couldn't find either a weapon or a bullet after an hour's search, I told the C.C. that I reckoned you'd like to get here today rather than tomorrow. And he agreed.'

Green had joined them. 'He was shot, you say?'

'Shot, yes. But we couldn't find the bullet.'

'Bullet hole in the wall, ceiling, floor? In a bit of furniture?'

Nicholson didn't like Green's patronizing tone. He said, stiffly: 'We looked everywhere.'

Green narrowed his eyes and opened his lips in disbelief. Masters forestalled any remark. He said: 'Perhaps we could start at the beginning.' Green took the hint, walked over to the fire and started warming his hands. Hill and Brant were with Crome at the sink. Nicholson said: 'There's not much to tell.' He set his mug down and lit a cigarette. Masters guessed he wasn't quite sure how and where to start.

'Crome was on early turn this morning. At eight o'clock he was standing on the corner of the square opposite here.'

'Where the main road runs out?'

'That's it. It's the best place for keeping an eye on the early heavy stuff going through. Anyhow, about five past eight . . .'

'Was it still dark?'

'Darkish. Sunrise was about a quarter to eight, but it's a dull day. Anyhow, one of the local builder's men ran up to Crome and told him they'd just found the parson dead in the school.'

'The school we passed on the way in?'

'That's the new school. This was the old one. Used to be the Church School. In use up to Christmas, but the Comprehensive opened in the new year, so the old one closed down.'

'What were the builders doing? Pulling it down?'

'No. It's been rented by the potato factory as a despatch store. They've got brickies and chippies in turning one classroom into offices and making a loading bay out of the school hall.'

Masters could see it in his mind's eye, using his own first school as a stage setting. An old building with a flagged hall that was too cold and draughty to be used as anything but a corridor. He remembered it with a little burst of nostalgia. How happy he'd been there. He used to ring the handbell—a coveted honour. He said: 'The workmen clocked in at eight and found the body?'

'That's right. It'd been empty since they left on Friday afternoon.'

'Was the school locked over the weekend?'

Nicholson grimaced in disgust. 'Was it hellers like! You'll see for yourself. The playground wall's been knocked down to let in the lorries and the wall of the school itself has been knocked out at the back to make the loading bay.'

'So anybody could get in and out as they wanted. And probably unseen.'

'If they wanted to. Certainly they could by dark. Mark you, there were some planks nailed up in the gap in the school wall, but they only had to be prised aside.'

Masters began to fill his pipe. He asked: 'Where's the body now?'

'Still there. Just as it was found.'

'What?'

Nicholson shrugged. 'When I knew you were coming up straight away I thought you'd like to see him just as we found him. The weather's as cold as any mortuary slab so I didn't think it would do any harm.'

He didn't say so, but Masters' opinion of Nicholson went up a few notches. He contented himself with: 'That was a useful idea. Had I known, I wouldn't have wasted time here.'

'No hurry. The electric's still on in the school so you'll have plenty of light.'

'What about the workmen? Are they still there?'

'They'd got some other job they could do so we let them collect their tools and push off. My sergeant's in charge at the school.'

Masters picked up his coat. He said: 'I suppose they nailed up the entrance because they'd left their tools in the school. Anything reported missing?'

'Nothing. I thought of that one.'

They moved towards the door. Green, behind them, said: 'Have we got anywhere to stay?'

Nicholson said: 'There's five pubs in Rooksby, but only one with any accommodation—the Goblin. We're not what you might call a holiday centre . . .' Masters shivered inwardly at the thought, '. . . but a few commercials come this way now and again. Binkhorst can let you have two singles and one double. All right?'

Masters going first down the stairs said: 'Who's Binkhorst? The publican? Is he foreign?'

'He's not, but his wife is. Italiano. You'll find a lot of foreign-sounding names in Rooksby. Dutch mostly. Like Vanden, our other constable here.'

Green said: 'Why?'

'They came over to do the draining ages ago. They made Rooksby their centre and settled here.'

Green said: 'So we're dealing with a crowd of Boers. I had a hunch they were something like that.' He turned to Crome, arriving last at the foot of the stairs. 'Who's the character called Perce who shoves a barrowful of buckets about the streets?'

'That'll be Percy Jonker, sir. He keeps the ironmonger's. He'd be fetching a load from his warehouse to the shop if you saw him.'

'I saw him. Ironmonger! Troublemonger more like. He'll be behind iron bars if he's not careful. Tell him to watch it or I'll shove his nose up his own backside and make a wheelbarrow trundle out of him.'

Masters asked: 'And who is Ted who drives a ten-tonner for the potato factory?'

'Ted Blount, sir. Our local boxer.'

'He looked a bit of a bruiser. And what, or where, is Barrett's?'

'Barrett's farm, sir. Big potato growers. If that's where Ted was going today he'd be in a hurry.'

'He was. But why?'

'They'll have opened up a clamp, sir, and they'll be wanting to get all the potatoes moved before night in case the frost sets in.'

They'd reached the car. Masters said to Nicholson: 'How far's the school?'

'About a couple of hundred yards.'

'In that case d'you mind if we walk? I'd like to see the village. Sergeant Brant can bring the car along. And I don't think there's any need for your constable to come.'

Crome was disappointed. He hung back as the others set off. Green didn't like the thought of being out in the cold wind, but he felt relieved he wouldn't have to drive in failing light through more narrow streets with the chance of ten-tonners bearing down on him from behind. Nicholson pointed out the Goblin facing across the square. Leaning against the wind they moved past the drab war memorial and out along the single pavement of the main road. Masters felt that not only the weather was depressing. On their side they passed little houses with doors opening directly from front rooms on to the narrow path. Across the road were death-trap shops lit by low-powered bulbs. Masters wondered whether the youngsters of Rooksby stuck to the place when they grew up or whether they swelled the belt-fed migration to the south-east. He decided the Dutch element would probably stay on, perpetuating their isolationist enclave, while the native British would flee to more congenial areas, glad to be free of drab, flat surroundings and dour neighbours.

They came to another crossroad: a replica of the spot where they had met Perce, except that here two of the corners were shop premises. A private grocer and the Co-op shop in direct competition. They turned left round a high wall of old bricks newly rebuilt. The nameplate said: Church Walk.

Nicholson broke the silence. 'This on the left is the vicarage garden. It stretches from here to the church.' Masters could just make out, forty or fifty yards away across the end of Church Walk, a lych-gate. Beyond that, a few bare trees silhouetted against a bit of sky a paler grey than the rest; and the heavy blur of a church tower. Nicholson added: 'The other side's all school property—or was.'

Masters crossed to look. The others followed. Behind a four-foot wall was what had once been the school garden. Ill-cared for and drear, even in the gathering gloom, the small plot divisions where children had laboured could still be made out. A wall divided the garden from the school itself. The main building stood about ten feet back from Church Walk, behind high iron railings on a dwarf footing. The narrow path to the playground behind ran between the garden wall and the gable end of the school. Masters stopped at the main gate and looked across at the vicarage opposite: a tall, greyish, nondescript house too big for present-day needs. He walked on, past the remainder of the school railings to the lych-gate. He noted that an unmetalled way, guarded by upright wooden posts to stop vehicles, ran off to the right between the walls of the churchyard and school. The church stood a hundred gloomy feet away. Too big ever to be filled these days. He guessed the churchyard was permanently fuller than the pews could ever be. A hummocky carpet of graves and broken stones with—strangely stark—a few early daffodils, golden in the gloom, being blown to an early death. Between the trunks of bare trees behind the church he could just make out the grey water of an overfull dyke poppling in the wind. He shivered mentally: cheerless and cold. He spared a moment to wonder if the dead vicar's last view of his church had been as full of foreboding as this.

He joined the others at the main gate. Brant had arrived in the car. Nicholson led the way round the side alley to the playground. Loads of sand, ballast and bricks were dumped on a still clearly marked-out netball pitch. The lean-to bicycle shed was housing hundredweight bags of cement. The back wall of the school had been roughly holed. A light shone out. Masters saw that two tall windows and the brick courses between and below them had gone. Wooden puncheons supported the gap. Between the puncheons the builders had nailed a crazy wall of old doors and worn floor boards. Some had been levered aside. Just inside the gap, out of the wind, was one of Nicholson's detective constables. He was standing six inches below the level of the playground. Silhouetted against the light he appeared deformed, with a great body on legs too short to support it.

Masters peered in. The wooden floor and joists of what had formerly been the school hall had been ripped out. The space below was half filled with hard core, ready for concreting. Nicholson asked: 'Where's Sergeant Chapman?'

'In the classroom, sir.'

There were obviously several classrooms: green doors with spherical brass handles, badly tarnished, led off the hall at both ends. Masters and Green followed Nicholson diagonally across the rubble. Nicholson opened one of the doors and stepped up into the room. Masters half expected to see rows of desks. Instead, the floor was littered with rolls of thermal padding for roofs; a neat heap of six by four plaster boards; and a several hundred foot run of heavy squared timber. Sergeant Chapman was sitting on a form at a makeshift table made from a blackboard resting on saw benches. He hadn't made it himself. Judging from the brewing gear, Masters guessed it was where the workmen wetted their tea. Nicholson asked: 'Anything new?'

Chapman got to his feet. He looked keen, but browned off. 'Nothing, sir. I've written up the workmen's statements and the doctor's verbal report. And I had a good scout round outside while it was still light. Nothing there besides building materials and junk. No blood anywhere apart from the wall. And no bullet inside here, either.'

Green said: 'These rolls of padding would conceal a bullet.' He sounded accusing. Chapman didn't like it. He said: 'I've been through them with a flea comb.'

Masters was looking round the room. It was just like one he'd known as a kid. He could have described it with his eyes shut. No ceiling. It ran, high roofed, up to an apex with brown painted heavy beams laid across at wall top level, tied by long metal bottle screws to the roof trusses. He remembered thinking how, as a little boy, he'd imagined himself climbing among them: but always his imagination had soared too high for his childish equilibrium, and he'd felt a stab of fear at the thought of the drop even though his feet had been firmly planted on the floor.

The joiners had already started putting up a false ceiling. Subsidiary struts of raw, white wood were nailed across the beams, waiting for plaster boards and the insulating material. Nicholson said in a whisper: 'They're lowering it so's they'll be able to keep it warm.' He was in the presence of death and it constrained him.

Masters asked, in a normal voice: 'Why heat a warehouse? Or does dried potato have to be kept warm?'

'Not warm. Dry. But that's not the point here. This room's being divided into offices.'

Green said: 'That explains those plates on the walls.'

Masters looked puzzled. 'Plates?'

'Those planks of wood nailed vertically. See? One plumb in the centre of each wall. They're there to take the ends of partitions.'

Nicholson said: 'That's right. And the vicar was standing dead in front of one of them when he was killed. Have a look.' Green opened his mouth to sneer at the unintentional pun and then thought better of it. They followed Nicholson. On the floor, near the wall opposite the door, was the body. It was covered with a sheet of heavy duty, milkily transparent polythene.

Sergeant Chapman drew the stiff sheet aside. Masters asked: 'What's his name?'

'Herbert James Parseloe. Known locally as Gobby Parseloe.'

Green asked why.

'Because he was always either speaking or eating at other people's expense.'

Masters asked: 'Not popular?'

'Not very. He was an outner, of course. Nobody who's not been born in Rooksby is ever really well received.'

Masters hitched his new trousers and squatted beside the dead man. He studied him carefully from top to toe. The bloodless face with the beard area covered in stubble. The thin hair, still mainly black, plastered down with solid brilliantine that still glistened, and though awry now, obviously worn dressed into a skimpy covering for the obvious bald patch. The meagre moustache, shaved too narrow for the depth of the upper lip, giving a downward, mean look to the thin mouth. The gold-rimmed spectacles the wrong shape for the face—too wide and too shallow to make them a congruent feature. The dog-collar with a faint rime of grubbiness along the upper edge which suggested it had been worn a day too long. The cassock, unbuttoned as far as the waist, but still held firm by a cord round the middle. Black corduroy trousers, pale grey nylon socks and slip-on shoes, dull and scuffed for want of polish.

There was blood about. Not much. Masters drew the stiff top of the cassock aside. Green said: 'Where's his black front?'

Because Green had been so pleased with himself about the plates on the walls, Masters said without looking up: 'Rabats are worn with jackets, not necessarily with cassocks.'

The shirt had a saucer-sized bloodstain with a small ragged hole near the top edge. Green said: 'He didn't bleed much.'

'I'd have thought there would have been more,' Nicholson said.

'If he died instantly, as he must have done, there'd only be one pump of blood left in the heart. About an eggcupful. It'd be forced down the artery and out. After that, nothing. His vest, shirt and cassock would soak it up easily.' With great care Masters moved the shirt front. The strands of the string vest were clogged, stiff and dry. A small, bluish, jagged hole showed up almost in the centre of the chest. He examined it closely without speaking. Green squatted beside him, frightened to miss anything. Nicholson said: 'What's up? Aren't you satisfied?'

Masters didn't answer immediately. He took a small plastic rule from his pocket and took a couple of measurements near the entrance wound. Then he asked: 'Is this the position he was in when he was found?'

'Not quite. The doctor had to examine him, so we had to move him a bit.'

'How much?'

'He wasn't on his back.' Chapman came over with a photograph. 'Like this. More on his side. At least his face was. See? And his chest was over frontwards.'

'But still in this spot?'

'Right there. We turned his top half over so that the doctor could get at his chest, but his legs didn't move much.'

Masters said: 'Can you put him back like he was?'

Chapman stepped forward slowly. He didn't like the job. Masters helped until Nicholson was satisfied. All they could now see of the features was the left-hand profile. In the middle of the back was a mess of gore, solidified, dark, unpleasant. Masters felt sick. The vomit actually reached his throat. It took conscious effort to keep it down. Green stared and then turned away, heaving. Masters, forcing himself to do it, used his rule to lay bare the crater. Nearly three inches in diameter and an inch deep. Only when he was satisfied he could have missed nothing did he straighten up, the rule dangling between finger and thumb.

Chapman said: 'There's a row of basins in the cloakroom.'

Masters, said simply: 'Thank you. Would you mind opening the doors for me?' He turned to Green. 'Ask Hill to bring the pHisoHex and nailbrush.'

Nicholson followed him out. 'What's this stuff—what d'you call it?'

'pHisoHex?' Nicholson nodded. 'It's an antibacterial skin cleanser. Surgeons use it in operating theatres. We carry a bottle in our bag for occasions like this.'

After he had scrubbed up and dried on the towel Hill had brought in, Masters returned to the classroom. 'Now,' he said, 'let's reconstruct the last few moments of his life. We think he was killed standing on the spot where he is now lying. Correct?'

Nicholson said: 'There aren't any signs that the body was moved after death, and the mess on the wall makes it sure. But there's no sign of any bullet hole, either.'

Masters edged round the body to look at the timber nailed to the wall. Just above the height of his stomach was a wide splodge of discoloration. He judged it to be the exact height of the vicar's wound. 'This has been wiped.'

Nicholson said: 'Of course it has. There was a great dollop of blood and snot there and I wanted to find the bullet.'

Masters peered closely. The unplanned, rough plank bore no sign of a bullet hole or pock mark of any kind. The bare brick wall on either side was clear and smooth except for discoloration. The blood, tissue, bone and shreds of clothing had been smeared downwards. There was no pattern left: just a few dark runnels of dried blood coursing down to the floor. He said to Green: 'There should have been two distinct splodges.'

Green stared for a moment and then said: 'How do you make that out?'

'If he was standing up close to the wall when he was shot, there would be a sort of recoil. His trunk would be forced a few inches away from the wall and there'd be one great splatter of blood behind him. His knees would have given slightly and he'd then have fallen back again, striking the wall with his wound a few inches lower down. This would leave another spatter—this time imprinted.'

Green said: 'That's right. The back of his cassock's got a ring of blood above the wound. I wondered where it came from. When he went backwards the second time, the spatter he'd made the first time got him higher up on the back of his shoulders.'

'And after that,' said Masters, 'I think his knees gave completely. He fell to the right, almost over on to his front.'

Nicholson asked: 'And you say he was dead at the time?'

Masters nodded. 'If he hadn't been dead he'd have staggered forward. But his feet didn't move from the wall.'

'It sounds right. Now p'raps you can tell me what happened to the bullet.'

'I can't,' Masters said. 'So I'm not going to worry my head about it just yet.'

'Not going to worry about it? When a bullet's gone right through a man from front to back and then disappeared into thin air?'

'There are plenty of other things to worry about. I'd like to have the body removed now. Can you arrange it?'

Nicholson nodded to Chapman who went towards the door. Masters called after him: 'Would you ask my two sergeants to come in, please?'

Hill and Brant needed no orders. They knew they were to inspect the classroom and everything in it for fingerprints and any suspicious items. They brought in the bags and photographic equipment and began their job. Masters said: 'I'd like to see the doctor who examined him.'

'Dr Barnfelt. He's the local G.P. and the police surgeon.' Nicholson looked at his watch. 'Half past six. He'll be in evening surgery now.'

'Good. We'll ring him.'

'No phone here. What about clocking in at the Goblin and phoning from there?'

Masters nodded and put on his coat. He said: 'Only one doctor in Rooksby?'

'Two. Barnfelt and his son in partnership.'

Green said: 'Are they outners?'

'No. The old man's father started the practice. He was born here, and so was his son.'

'So they're O.K. people round here?'

'The best. The village thinks the world of them both.'

Masters asked: 'What do you think of them?'

Nicholson said, off-handedly: 'They're all right.'

Chapter Two

They made their way back to the village square and the Goblin. As they went, blown by the wind in the wild half-light of blue street lamps and haloed moon, Masters said to Nicholson: 'Did you interview the family?'

'There's no wife. He's a widower. His youngest daughter's there but she's daft, so she was no good to me.'

'How many daughters are there? Three or four?'

'Two. The oldest one works in Peterborough. She's a teacher. The youngest one's at home. She's a cretin or a moron or something.'

Nicholson's lack of distinction between comparative and superlative annoyed Masters. He thought no senior policeman could afford to be so imprecise. He said: 'So we know nothing about the Parseloe family and their reactions. Right! I'll attend to that myself tomorrow. That leaves us very little more to discuss at the moment. So, sir, I don't think there's any great need for you to introduce us at the Goblin. You've already done your stint for today, and I don't think there's a lot more we can usefully do this evening.'

'I thought you were going to the doctor's.'

'Alone.' Masters was quite firm. He wanted to be rid of Nicholson. Free to tackle the problem in his own way. He said: 'I hope you'll arrange the inquest and all the etceteras. I shan't want to interfere with those at all.'

Nicholson could feel the pressure, but couldn't counter it. Masters was kicking him out. For a moment he felt angry, then nothing more than a reluctance to sever himself from the case. He'd heard of Masters long before today. Would have liked to watch him in action. Although come to think of it, he had already seen him in action. He'd been pretty sharp over that bit about the body rebounding. And he'd shown he'd got guts when he'd stirred up the gore in that back wound. Nicholson slowed as they neared the police station. He said: 'Why waste a tanner at the pub? I'll leave you here and ring Barnfelt to tell him you're coming.'

'Tell you what, Super,' said Green. 'You ring the Doc and then step over to the Goblin to tell us what time he can see the Chief. While he's gone, you and me can have a jar together.'

Nicholson said: 'Thanks. I'll take you up on that. See you in five minutes.'

Green grinned to himself in triumph. He'd spiked Masters' guns. Foiled his efforts to get rid of Nicholson at the earliest possible moment. Green knew Masters would have noted it, and satisfaction warmed him inside like a shot of neat whisky. Masters, head down against the wind, made for the curtained squares of red light that were the front of the Goblin.

Binkhorst was fifty, or thereabouts. A nondescript, colourless man. He was in the saloon bar. Masters didn't like waistcoats and shirt sleeves together. Particularly double-breasted waistcoats with lapels and shirt sleeves with garters. He said: 'I believe you're expecting four of us. Two of us are here now. The others will arrive later. Please book me in and arrange for all four of us to have dinner at half past eight.'

Binkhorst said: 'It'll have to be before that. Mrs Binkhorst likes to serve at half past seven. Then she's free to help in the bars later.'

Masters said to Green: 'Ring up the nearest decent hotel and arrange bookings for all four of us. Give them my name and say we'll be in for dinner at half past eight.' He turned to Binkhorst. 'Inspector Green would like to use your phone.'

Binkhorst said: 'Whoa! Give me a chance to see what I can do first. She won't like it, but I can ask.' Masters was puzzled. For a moment Binkhorst had given him the distinct impression that they were unwelcome. Now he seemed to have changed his mind.

'You mean you'd like us to stay? Good. We'd like to. As long as it's understood that I shall not be dictated to. The hours my staff and I keep are often irregular, and I like a pub that's run for my convenience, not vice versa.'

Binkhorst went through to the kitchen. Green had moved away. He hated standing by when Masters was high-hatting somebody, as he always did when he was crossed or he thought his importance wasn't fully appreciated. Green had a moment of remorse. If he hadn't annoyed Masters by inviting Nicholson for a drink, the Chief might have let Binkhorst off a bit more lightly. Not for the first time he realized Masters was not an easy man to get the better of for long. He felt threads of animosity against Masters crawling like spiders over his entire body.

The saloon bar was empty except for the two of them. Masters looked about him. The floor was uneven red tiles. The fire bright. The furniture reproduction oak, well polished. The brasses modern, but shiny. The ceiling low. No beams, either real or mock. The place appealed. It was snug and warm. It needed more lights in the corners, but it made him feel sorry he had to go out again.

Nicholson came in. Green offered them both drinks. Masters declined. Binkhorst reappeared when Green rang. He said: 'It's fixed for half past eight.' Masters thought the landlord looked abashed. He half smiled to reassure him. Nicholson said: 'It'll take you no more than five minutes to get to Doc's place,' and proceeded to explain the way. Masters thanked him and said: 'I think you ought to keep a man in the school tonight and tomorrow. After that we should be able to lay off. And as far as I'm concerned your men can stay inside the classroom, out of the cold.'

'You don't think they'll ruin any evidence?'

Masters fastened his coat. 'Not after Hill and Brant have been over it.' He said good night and turned to go, saying quietly to Green as he passed: 'There's likely to be more evidence to pick up in here. Keep your ears open. I want to know what the locals think about things.'

Dr Barnfelt's waiting-room was drab. Bentwood chairs on brown linoleum. A gas fire with one broken clay, sputtering drearily. A green pull-down blind over the window. No receptionist. No instructions for patients except to keep medicines out of the reach of children. Masters felt sunk in a sea of misery. If he were to stay long in that atmosphere he'd begin to imagine he had every malady known to man. A bell rang. A blowsy woman grunted: 'Oo's next for young doctor?' An elderly man with chronic bronchitis—or worse—shuffled out. The blowsy woman said: 'Sid won't be with us for long if these winds keep up. What 'e needs is camphorated an' a brown paper vest. Not a bottler jollop.' Another bell rang—a different note. 'That's t'owd doctor. My turn.' She waddled out towards the surgery. Masters settled down to wait. Wanted a pipe. Had it half packed before a lad said: 'You can't smoke in 'ere, mister.'

Dr Frank Barnfelt, the senior partner and local police surgeon, amazed Masters from the moment of meeting. Masters hadn't known what to expect, but it certainly wasn't this man. A fifty-year-old don in rimless pince-nez with a bootlace over his right ear running down to a small gold clip on his right lapel. A full head of sandy hair going very grey, neatly parted on the right side. A Hitler moustache, also very grey. Full coloured cheeks. Pale blue eyes, intelligent and twinkling. A light fawn Harris tweed jacket. Grey flannel trousers with no fore-and-aft creases. Masters guessed they'd been made in the round on purpose, and ever thereafter ironed on a sleeve board. Highly polished brown boots with a patina as deep as a well.

Masters hated shaking hands. He hated it more than ever this time. Barnfelt's skin was dry and rasping on his own. The fingers bony. The knuckles dressed with some form of yellow lacquer, like a second skin. Masters imagined the cold weather had chapped and cracked his hands, softened by too much washing and scrubbing up after seeing patients. His voice was high pitched; neither girlish nor mincing, but noticeably acute, with a slight cackle in the cadences. He said: 'I was expecting to see you, even before Nicholson rang.' He grinned, showing a set of false teeth that some dental mechanic had spent time on to achieve a very natural colour. Masters felt pleased at the sight. He hated china clappers.

Masters said: 'It's good of you to see me after so long a day. You started—over at the school—shortly after eight, they tell me, and you haven't finished yet.'

'It's a twenty-four hour job—like yours.'

'We manage a little time off occasionally.'

'So do we. My son and I take turn and turn about. He was off this last weekend.'

'Off? Out of Rooksby?'

'No. But off duty and free to go out as he liked. Like last night. There was a bridge party at the home of some friends of ours—the de Hooch's. Peter is fond of a rubber of bridge.'

'Isn't your son married?'

Barnfelt frowned slightly. 'Not yet.'

'Girl friends?'

Masters could see this was a question the doctor would have preferred to avoid. The frown grew deeper. So far, Masters had been making nothing more than idle conversation, but he always pressed a point that seemed to unsettle the person questioned. He persisted: 'Has there been a tiff?'

'I fear so. Yes. A tiff. Everything was going quite smoothly up to a fortnight or three weeks ago, since when I've not heard of April, or seen her.'

'April?'

'April Barrett.'

'The potato farmer's daughter?'

Barnfelt opened his mouth in amazement. 'You learn fast, Chief Inspector. At what time did you arrive in Rooksby?'

Masters felt pleased with himself. He pretended to pass it off. He said airily: 'Oh, three or four hours ago, now,' as if he were accustomed to learning everything there was to know about a place the size of Rooksby in the time it would take most people to eat a boiled egg.

'And now you've come to me to . . . er . . . increase your knowledge still further? Yes?'

'Strictly professionally. To discuss the wounds on the vicar's body.'

Barnfelt rubbed his hands together. They made a harsh sound. His voice sounded strange above it. 'Haematomata and induration?' he asked. Masters had the feeling he was being treated as another medical man being asked for a second opinion. But the matter was too abstruse for him. He didn't know the proper cries. He ignored the technical terms and decided to guess. He said: 'It's a decidedly odd wound.'

The doctor grinned. 'Nicholson was looking for a bullet, wasn't he?'

'And you think he was wasting his time?'

'Not entirely. But I'd have been looking for a projectile somewhat different from a conventional revolver or pistol bullet.'

'If he had done as you suggest, would he have found a projectile?'

'I can't say, because I don't know what sort of a projectile it was.'

Masters said: 'What makes you so sure it was not a bullet?'

'The lacerated edges of the entry wound.'

'Atypical?'

'Decidedly. Bullets go in cleanly and come out messily. This projectile came out messily, all right, but it went in messily, too.'

'So it wasn't a bullet? Not even a dumdum?'

The doctor said: 'Dumdums are made to stop a man dead in his tracks by blowing a hole the size of a soup plate in his back. But they still go in neatly at the front, because only the tapered nose is nicked. It flattens out later if it meets any opposition hard enough to open out the cut.'

Masters said: 'I know the theory. I've never seen it put into practice, fortunately.'

'Then you'll realize that marked laceration indicates a projectile other than a bullet. Yes?'

'You mentioned this to Nicholson?'

'I pointed out to him that there were lacerations up to a quarter of an inch long round the periphery. The points were bent inwards, like the cogs on an anti-vibration washer. They were very easy to see.'

'And he thought your observations unimportant?'

'He regards me, I fear, merely as a sadly out-of-date, country G.P.'

Masters thought Barnfelt sounded sorry about it. He decided to see whether Nicholson's view was correct. He said: 'In many bullet wounds the flesh around the entry stands proud. Why not this time?'

Barnfelt put the tips of his skinny fingers together. He said: 'The periphery is only proud if the skin has been forcibly depressed beforehand. When this happens, as when a conventional bullet strikes, the elastic skin tissue reasserts itself after being forced inwards. It bounces outwards and stays put. Here we have the opposite effect. The skin has been forced outwards and then drawn downwards.'

'Outwards?'

'Not vertically away from the body. No projectile forcing an entry could do that. But it could be forced outwards to widen the circle—as it were, thus producing a similar effect. The skin tissue was being drawn in after being forced outwards . . .'

'Understood,' said Masters. 'The projectile must have been wider at some point along its length than its general width—not counting a tapered point, if there was one.'

Barnfelt nodded. 'That is my professional belief. And as I was a regimental M.O. in the line during the last war, I am not unacquainted with G.S. wounds. I think my opinion is borne out by the appearance of the exit wound. The projectile did not flatten as a dumdum would have done, but the broader part of its calibre caused a three-inch wound which you doubtless examined.'

Master was nearly sick at the mention of it. He nodded. The doctor offered him a cigarette which he refused. He said: 'You've explained the lacerations, doctor. But earlier you mentioned . . . what were the words? . . . haematomata and induration. What are they? Anything to do with bruising?'

Barnfelt smiled. A little smile that showed his teeth. 'Is that guesswork, Chief Inspector? Or have you some good reason for asking? Haematomata has to do with bruises.'

Masters said: 'Good enough. I know the thump of a bullet causes bruising in the vicinity of its entry hole.'

'And marked induration—hardening and bruising,' said Barnfelt. 'The bluish area around the wound is always harder, less elastic.'

Masters nodded. 'I saw you'd bathed the area. Did you notice anything peculiar about the bruising of the chest?'

'I did. But I wouldn't have expected you to have done so, too. You must be half a pathologist in your own right.'

'I'm not a forensic expert. But I use my eyes. There was a very faint, larger bruise around the wound. A bruise about two inches square.'

'Quite right. I should say that whatever blow caused that bruise was struck with a square object, such as the end of one of the pieces of timber lying in the classroom.'

'Do blows from square weapons leave square bruises?'

'Not normally, because extravasation—that's seepage of blood from tiny damaged vessels—spreads like a stain into surrounding tissue and blurs the edges of the area that has been struck.'

'I could make out a distinct square.'

'So could I.'

'And what does that tell us?'

'That the blow was struck, I should say, within a minute of death.'

'Before or after?'

'Definitely before. The extravasation had no time to spread before the circulation stopped. That's why the bruise retained its shape.'

Masters felt a surge of pleasure. He'd got a very definite, significant fact. He hardly heard Barnfelt say: 'What do you think of my idea that he was prodded with a length of timber?'

Masters looked at him for a moment and shook his head. Barnfelt opened his blue eyes in surprise. Masters said: 'I took measurements. The bullet hole was plumb in the middle of the bruise. It'd be an amazing coincidence if—well, if lightning were to strike in exactly the same place twice within a minute.'

'I see.'

He sounded deflated. Masters felt sorry. Barnfelt had helped. He ought to be given a crumb of comfort. Masters said: 'You put a bomb under your own idea yourself, you know.'

'Did I?'

'Could a murderer prod a man with a baulk of timber, put the timber down, hold his victim in place, draw a gun and shoot him, all within a minute?'

'He could. But I agree it would take a bit of quick action. Especially as the victim would be bound to struggle.'

'That's what I think. It'd be extremely unlikely. I can't visualize it happening. And when the shot found the exact centre of the area bruised . .

.' He spread his hands. 'Speed and accuracy like that would be impossible.' He rose to go. Almost as if a passing thought had struck him he asked: 'By the way, what time would you say he was killed?'

Barnfelt smiled. 'I've been working it out as accurately as I can. My answer is before ten o'clock last night.'

'No closer?'

Barnfelt shook his head. 'But don't forget it was Sunday. Parseloe would have been in church conducting Evensong until seven thirty or thereabouts, wouldn't he?'

'So I've got a two and a half hour bracket.'

'Unless you can cut it down in some way. Don't parsons cash up the takings after the service with the church wardens? That's the sort of thing you've got to ferret out.'

Masters thanked him gravely for the advice.

*

Hill and Brant were packing up when Masters joined them. He asked: 'Anything?'

Hill said: 'Not a skerrick. I've never known a place with less to offer. No decipherable prints on the door handles or anywhere else. No footmarks. No bullets. No bullet holes. No nothing.'

'Come back for dinner,' Masters said.

Brant said: 'I'd like to know what happened to that bullet.'

'I know,' Hill replied. 'He was shot with a bullet made of ice, which melted as soon as it'd done its stuff. No marks left on the wall and nothing on the floor except a few unnoticed drops of water. How's that for a theory that fits?'

Masters said: 'Hurry up or we'll be late. They're only keeping our meal till eight thirty as a special favour.'

'Let's hope it's worth waiting for,' Hill said.

*

It was. They were all agreed. Roast pork with good crackling that Green crunched loud and long. They were served by Mrs Binkhorst. While she was out Green said: 'So she's the Eyetie. Gone to seed a bit like most Wops.'

Masters didn't think so. He placed her in the late forties. She was tall for a Latin; more heavily boned than usual. But her legs were still a good shape in high-heeled red shoes. Her figure was corseted, smoothing the outlines of the black dress round her buttocks and holding the full bosom high under a cascade of white nylon lace. The skin on hands and face was still brown and taut. The hair had been dyed so that it was unnaturally black, too soft and matt in colour—like soot. Long earrings dangled, hard and bright. But Masters felt she had a presence. And there was no doubt she could cook, too. He told her so as she collected the empty plates.

'The pig that breaks its leg is always good,' she said with very little accent.

'Breaks its leg?'

'You do not know it? It is always said in Rooksby.'

'What is?' Green said.

'When the war was on and the farmers were not allowed to kill their pigs for themselves. If they wanted more food they killed a forbidden pig. They told the food men that the pig had broken its leg and had to be killed. They always ate much in Rooksby and laughed at the regulations. Now always when they kill pigs they say they have broken a leg. They tasted good when there was a war. They taste good now. Not from a butcher.'

Masters said: 'You were here before the war?'

'I married six months before. I was seventeen. Some people did not like me when the war was on.'

'But they do now?'

She shrugged. 'They call me Gina and come every night to the Goblin. What more?'

'You don't sound very happy about it to me. Have you any children?'

'Maria.'

'How old?'

'Twenty-eight.' She paused a moment and then almost sobbed: 'A pretty, pretty girl. And not married. It is not good. She should be married before now. With children.'

When she brought the ice cream cake she was more composed. 'You will see Maria in the saloon bar. She serves there every night among the men. All of them like her, but she does not get married. I do not know what the men are doing today.'

Green said: 'The same as they always did. Only more so.' And after Mrs Binkhorst had gone he added: 'Little Maria won't play, if you ask me. She serves the men, but she won't let them serve her. She'll be a Catholic most likely—her mother being an Eyetie.'

Masters said: 'Why don't you make a point of finding out?'

'Why?'

'Because it'll be one way of starting people gossiping. I want to get the atmosphere of this place. Start with Maria. You can forget her once you've got going—unless you think there's something nasty in the Goblin's woodshed.'

Green stretched and yawned. It was a sign he didn't think much of Masters' orders. He said: 'Where shall I start? In the spit and sawdust? I take it you'll do the saloon bar yourself?'

'Hill and I will take the public bar for half an hour just to see how it goes. You and Brant do the saloon.'

Green was surprised. Masters didn't usually take the rough end of a job without good reason. He wondered what the reason was this time. Masters knew he was wanting to know, but didn't enlighten him. The public bar was likely to have more youngsters in it. They might not take kindly to Green who would be more at home among the older—and probably more garrulous—saloon frequenters.

Hill wandered into the saloon. He was back inside a minute. He said to Masters: 'She's some bird, all right. Legs just a bit skinny for a micro, but still a good shape. And her face isn't too bad, either. One of those sultry Italians. But what lips! They look as though they'd have a kiss on 'em like a vacuum cleaner.'

Masters led the way into the public bar. There were seven or eight young men and two or three older ones present. Binkhorst was behind the bar. He seemed surprised to see Masters. Masters guessed why. They'd been discussing him, believing him unlikely to come to this room. Nobody said anything at first. Hill broke the ice. He said in a voice that sounded unnaturally loud in the silence: 'No women this side? Fair do's, landlord. What you want is a bouncing barmaid. I'll bet that'd be popular.'

'Nay it wouldn't,' said one of the older men. 'Most o' these young'uns come here to get away from women, and us old'uns don't care.'

Masters said: 'That doesn't sound typical.'

'It is though. They're all married, this lot. Left their lasses at home minding the bairns.'

Masters was genuinely surprised. He guessed some of the youths were less than nineteen. If it hadn't been for the long sideboards they could truly have been taken for beardless.

One of them said: 'Aw, shut up, dad. You blow too much.'

'Do I? An' what do you lot do? Aye! Go on! Start playing darts while I'm talking to you. It's a pity you didn't stick to darts a year since.' He turned to Masters. 'You're a detective, I hear. Well, I bet you've never met any place like this. I'm telling you that few lasses in Rooksby ever reach the age of seventeen without being wed force-put. There 'asn't been a wedding here this last twenty year, I doubt, but the girl's been big-bellied at the altar. 'As there, Matthew?'

The man appealed to nodded. 'Right, 'Arold. These little lasses 'as to get married, an' before the first youngster's born they're fighting cat an' dog with their men.' He leaned towards Masters. 'But what I don't understand is these lasses 'aving no spirit after they're wed. They let these lads come out every night while they sit home with the kids. Slavery it is.'

A tall young man reached for his beer and interrupted: 'Stop your chelping, Matthew. You don't know what you're talking about.'

'Oh, don't I? Look at you. Not yet twenty-one and saddled with two kids. And you not earning enough to buy salt for your spuds, let alone drinking Double Diamond.'

The youth made no reply. Masters thought he could see misery in the face. These boys and their young wives were missing life. Drinking to avoid reality. Unable to afford this chosen escape from responsibility. Poverty the banana skin on the threshold of their married lives. The thought was as depressing as the village. He said: 'Why don't you bring your wives out occasionally? They might like it here.'

'That's the trouble. They might like it too much. Then where'd we be?' There was no animosity in the reply. Just surliness.

Old Harold said: 'Sittin' home some nights, where you should be now.'

The youth returned to his game. Masters looked towards the bar. Binkhorst was dipping and wiping glasses, apparently paying no attention to the conversation. He was preoccupied. But every so often he glanced at Masters and Hill as though they were the subject of his thoughts. Masters wondered why. Was it a natural distrust of policemen? Was it dislike occasioned by his insistence on a late meal? It might be worth probing a little. He said to Harold: 'The landlord's daughter is still unmarried, I hear.'

'Aye, she is that. Proper old maid through no fault of her own.'

'Really? I heard she was an attractive girl.'

'Right enough—in a foreign sort of way. Her mother's kept her what we would call tethered to the table leg, but what you might call tied to her apron strings.'

Hill said: 'Kept an eye on her so she didn't end up like the rest of the girls in Rooksby, did she?'

'Aye. But too much. Never gave the lass a bit o' freedom when she was a young'un. Loosened up a bit lately. Bought her one of these mini cars of her own, and looking round for somebody to take her off their hands a bit desperate like now, I reckon. 'Course, there's talk about her.'

Masters said: 'Such as what?'

Harold's eyes seemed to glaze over. He clammed up. Masters sensed the old man felt he'd said too much. Masters didn't press him. Pretended to ignore the lack of response. The simple fact that the old man had dried up told him enough. Here was something to look into. It might end in nothing more than village gossip. It might go further. He couldn't tell—yet. He changed the subject abruptly. Often a good tactic when the person questioned is very anxious to do so. Out of sheer relief they might be more forthcoming on the new topic. Masters asked Harold: 'What did you think of the vicar?'

'Gobby Parseloe?'

Masters nodded. He said: 'I'm surprised you haven't mentioned him before now. His death must have caused some excitement and chatter in Rooksby.'

'I dunno.' Harold seemed disinclined to speak. Masters nodded to Hill to refill glasses—Harold's and Matthew's, as well as their own. The fresh beer help to lubricate tongues. Harold said: 'We ain't said ower much about it.'

'Why not?'

'We weren't ower fond. Mind, I'm not what you might call a churchgoer. Nor's Matthew, are you, Matthew?'

'Parson being an outner,' said Matthew, as though that explained whatever shortcomings Parseloe may have had, and those of Matthew, too, to account for his lack of attendance at church. 'No, we weren't ower fond o' Gobby. There's been talk about him, too.'

Masters said smugly: 'I'm very pleased to see—and hear—that there's no idle gossip about his death.'

Harold said: 'Gossip?' as though it were something he'd never encountered. 'Nay, no gossip.'

To Masters it sounded like a warning to Matthew to say no more. Masters wondered why. Would they be willing to say more if bought with beer? Or were these two oldsters saying no more in order to protect—

whom? Of course! To protect a local. An outner had been murdered. So what? All locals stick together for self-preservation. The law of the jungle. Masters wondered whether Harold and Matthew actually knew who the murderer was or whether instinct was making them cagey in the interests of the herd at large. He said: 'You're very wise not to gossip.'

'Keep your own council an' live a day longer,' said Matthew.

'That's true enough,' said Hill. 'But we've got to find out something about the vicar. To help us, I mean. Haven't we, Chief?'

Harold looked at Hill for a moment. He said: 'I doubt you won't hear much good about Gobby. But if you're set on it, talk to Arn Beck and Jan Wessel and a few like them. They'll tell you a thing or two, perhaps—if you're lucky.'

Masters looked across at Binkhorst. The landlord was standing with his back to them, in the small doorway that connected behind the counters of the two bars. Binkhorst was talking. Masters strained his ears to listen. '. . . you get to bed early tonight. Get off now and take something for that headache. And tell your mother to come and take over as you go up.' Masters couldn't hear the reply. He felt sorry he wouldn't be seeing the fair Maria after all, tonight. But that didn't alter his plan to join Green. He said to Harold: 'Do the men you mentioned ever come into the Goblin?'

'As like as not they're in the saloon now.' Harold finished his drink and added: 'Arn Beck used to be a churchwarden till he had a row with Gobby.'

*

Green and Brant were in separate parties, but both seemed well dug in. The saloon regulars seemed less inhibited than the mixture of youth and age in the public bar. Articulate middle-age—more prosperous than next door—gave a different atmosphere. Here there was social interest in the presence of a team from Scotland Yard. Green was cashing in on it. Where Masters had been paying to listen, Green was being plied with liquor. Masters wondered how much he'd learned—if anything.

When Masters entered, Green looked up for a moment and then continued with his conversation. Brant signalled Masters over. Brant said: 'This is Mr de Hoke—spelt Hooch—which seems a good name to meet in a pub, don't you think?'

Masters said: 'The bridge champion?'

de Hooch stared for a moment and then said: 'I'm not exactly a champion, but I like the game. My missus is the fiend. She practically dresses herself on her winnings. But how the devil did you know we play?'

'Nothing to it,' said Masters. 'No magic. I heard you'd been having a party last night.'

'Not a party. Just one table. Jan and Sue Wessel, my missus and me.'

Masters said: 'Do many others in Rooksby play?'

'We can manage about four tables when we have a match. Mostly us old'uns—like Jan, myself and Stan Barrett with our wives and a few youngsters like Peter Barnfelt—he's one of our doctors—and his fiancée, April Barrett—Stan's daughter.'

Masters said: 'It sounds like a real family party. Husbands, wives, fiancées.'

de Hooch pursed his lips. 'Not always. Bridge is a funny game. It causes more rows between friends than amateur theatricals. Talk about temperament over playing a hand! And post-mortems when it's all over! I can tell you it often parts husband from wife.'

'And presumably causes rifts between sweethearts.'

de Hooch said: 'Now I wonder how you came to say that? I should have said that young Peter and April were far too sensible to let a poor call at bridge upset them. But they've stopped seeing each other for—oh—for about a fortnight or three weeks now, just because April miscounted aces in a four-five no-trump call. I must say it puzzled me that they should have had a tiff at the time, but for it to carry on so long, with no sign of reconciliation in sight, has me beat. It really does. What'll you have? A whisky?'

Masters stayed just long enough with de Hooch to make it appear that he was neither scrounging drinks nor picking brains, and then left him to Brant and Hill. Green looked up as Masters approached. 'Mr Beck and Mr Wessel. Detective Chief Inspector Masters.'

'I've heard of you both,' said Masters, shaking hands. 'Mr Wessel, you're a bridge player, and Mr Beck, you're not. Is that right?'

Wessel was long-faced, long-nosed and loose-jowled, with carefully parted black hair and rimless spectacles. Masters would have put him down as more of a poker player than a bridge addict. He said: 'I can see Henry de Hooch has been talking. Parading our faults and weaknesses. An insurance manager ought to be more discreet, don't you think?' There was a twinkle in his eye as he spoke. Masters said: 'The more indiscreet people are, the more I like it, generally. But I must confess I sifted very little condemnatory evidence out of an account of the doings of the local bridge players. Nothing to make me think I'll be able to go home in the morning, for instance.'

Wessel grinned: 'So you've come over here to see what you can glean from us?'

'If you've anything of interest to tell me.'

'I'm the local lawyer. I get paid to keep my lips sealed.'

'Pity. However, my main reason for approaching you is to ask Mr Beck for a short character study of the late vicar. I like to know something about the people whose deaths I investigate, and as I've heard Mr Beck was a churchwarden at one time, I thought I might get a factual picture from him—if he'd care to help me.'

Beck said: 'What sort of thing do you want to know, Mr Masters?' It was like the sound of joyous bells to Masters to hear somebody say that. It was as if Beck had said: 'I know a lot that will be of help to you. You can have it all if you'll start me off at the right place and then let me keep going.' Masters knew the importance of the right question. Beck sounded sure of himself. Knew he had knowledge to impart, but was not aware which bits would be wheat and which chaff. Masters said: 'I've heard that the late vicar was not as well thought of in Rooksby as he might have been. This may be at variance with your own opinion—as his churchwarden. It may even be coloured by the fact that he was not a native of Rooksby. Would you care to put me right?'

Beck said: 'De mortuis . . .'

Masters said: 'That as good as confirms that he wasn't well thought of.'

'You're quick to draw conclusions.'

'Shall we say I notice straws in the wind?'

'And are adept at verbal fencing.' Beck was portly. A soft face, full and pink, that seemed to run back over his bald head. The hair still left at the sides was clean-white and soft. The eyes were big and kind. The shirt was of soft material, not firm enough to hold the collar in shape, but comfortable looking. At least the large knot of a Cambridge blue tie nestled snugly between the rounded ends. Beck was, Masters thought, prosperous, kindly, and pretty sharp. Just the chap for a churchwarden. Could put his hand in his pocket, could help people, and couldn't be bamboozled. This thought made Masters pause. Beck was obviously not a great admirer of Parseloe. Had the vicar tried to bamboozle him? It was worth a shot.

'May I know your business or profession, Mr Beck?'

'I'm an accountant.'

Masters grinned. He said: 'And as such you weren't prepared to have the financial wool pulled over your eyes? Or am I completely off net?'

'You're bang on net. Financial wool! I like that.'

'Golden Fleece,' murmured Wessel. 'I'm taking a lesson in something. I don't know what. Probably semantics. But I could have sworn I was seeing the art of second sight practised.'

Masters said: 'Could I know what worried you, Mr Beck?'

'Worried me?'

'I'm assuming that you were so dissatisfied with some of the financial dealings of either the church or its vicar that you resigned as churchwarden.'

'That's right. I did. But I wasn't worried. I was downright angry.'

'Would you please tell me the cause of your anger?'

Beck shrugged. 'You'll think it unimportant, I daresay. But the church is like anything else. Once you become closely connected with it, particularly in a responsible position like that of warden, you find lots of time to devote to it that you didn't know you had before. This is a sure sign that you are, in the modern idiom, becoming integrated. Or as I would put it, involved and interested.'

Masters said: 'So that a relatively minor matter assumes the proportions of a major issue?'

'Correct. What seemed important to me may seem trivial to you.'

'Perhaps you would let me be the judge.'

'Willingly. It was this way. I was responsible for the church accounts. There are several funds, but the amounts going through them in my day were so small they were easy to keep straight just as long as the system was adhered to.' While Beck was speaking Green had called for refills. When Beck paused to acknowledge his Guinness, Masters said: 'What system?'

'There's a church hall. It's hired out for dances, Girl Guide meetings, Mothers' Union teas—you know the sort of thing. Any private person or any club in Rooksby can hire it whether they are affiliated to the church or not. The hiring, or should I say the diary, was kept by the vicar, as he was usually available to make the bookings. But payment was supposed to be made to me as treasurer. For the most part this was understood by people who were in the habit of hiring the hall regularly, but once or twice, people unfamiliar with the system paid the vicar direct.'

'And he pocketed the dibs?'

'Just so. And gave no receipts and conveniently forgot to forward them. Once or twice I was embarrassed through asking for payment from some organization or for some function, only to be told that the fees had been paid and that I hadn't forwarded a legal receipt. This was not only distasteful to me, but distinctly bad from a personal business point of view.'

'The vicar may have just been forgetful.'

'That is the charitable view, Mr Masters. The view I took in the first few instances. But it happened too often—in fact, always—for me to hold that view for long. Remember I'm a sceptic about forgetfulness when it is of financial benefit to the one who forgets. I had such trouble in prising the money out of him on a number of occasions that I had special leaflets printed. They were given to every organizer who hired the hall and told them to pay me and me only.'

Masters said: 'Padre Parseloe wouldn't like that.'

'He didn't. But, you know, I believe he had such a tip about himself that he thought I'd swallowed his explanations whole. At any rate under me the funds were solvent and that must have saved him some trouble.'

They sat silent for a moment or two, until Wessel said: 'The Chief Inspector ought to have the rest, Arn.'

Masters jerked to attention. 'I'm sorry. I was just digesting what you'd told me. Contrary to your belief, I found it most interesting and important.'

'You're sure?'

'Mr Beck, people are usually murdered for some reason. Oh, I know there are some killings we call motiveless, but there is always a reason—either in the character of the victim or of his murderer. I don't know the murderer in this case—yet. Don't you think it's logical for me to concentrate on the victim whose identity I do know? There's at least a fifty-fifty chance of the reason for his murder lying within his own character.'

'That's how you work, is it?' Beck sounded more interested. Wessel leaned forward over the small table, full of empty glasses and white cardboard mats. 'You make it sound easy. It isn't, I'm sure. But I can see your ploy.'

'You get a nose for it in our game,' Green said. 'If somebody talks, you've got facts. If somebody refuses to talk, you've got grounds for suspicion. And if somebody tells lies it's like reading mirror writing, but you've got the message even if it is all arsey-tarsey. The witness I don't like's the half-and-halfer. Half fact, half fiction. Sorting one of them out's a work of art—and that's where your nose comes in. You smell your way from lie to truth like a dog sniffing out trees from lamp-posts in Quality Street. And it's just as nasty, I can tell you.'

Beck smiled. His cheeks dimpled. He looked like a cherub. He said: 'So you'd like to know why I resigned?'

Masters said: 'Please.'

'I don't know how much you know about the church, but you've probably heard it's pretty short of parsons in some areas. Or it was, a few years ago. Perhaps the situation is better now. I don't know. But at the time I was warden, quite a number of the small villages round here, all poor livings, were without incumbents. The Bishop did the obvious thing. He gave the vicars of more fortunate parishes the responsibility for arranging services in churches where there were no parsons.'

'I don't see how even God-botherers could be in two places at once.'

'That's just the point, Mr Green,' Beck said. 'They couldn't. So unless the churches concerned were so close that a parson could get from one to the other with no loss of time, an alternative way had to be found. And the alternative was to use lay preachers.'

'Was Parseloe given a second church?' Masters asked.

Beck replied: 'Three more. Two where he was supposed to arrange one service each Sunday, and another where he had to have a service once a fortnight. Now this was extremely fortunate for him because it meant that one lay preacher could work up one sermon each week and deliver it in one church in the morning and in the other in the evening. A second lay preacher was only required once a fortnight for the other church, so this was fairly easy to arrange. But the first man was quite hard worked, as you can imagine.'

'Parseloe found a volunteer?'

'A very good man. One of the County's travelling librarians. Not a well paid man, but well read, and a keen churchgoer. Parseloe used him good and proper. This man used to borrow a little car each Sunday to get to the churches, but he had to provide the petrol himself. After a time he approached me and said that the cost of the petrol was becoming a burden, so as treasurer I made him a grant of a few shillings a week to cover the cost. He was extremely grateful.' Beck smiled. 'But I'm a business man, Mr Masters. I didn't see why our church here should bear this cost and so I approached the treasurers of the other churches concerned.' He suddenly looked like an indignant cherub. 'Imagine my surprise when I was told by these men that they were already paying our vicar three guineas a week each for providing the services.'

Green whistled. Masters' face settled heavily. He began to fill a pipe ponderously. He gritted: 'Go on, Mr Beck.'

'I was on to Parseloe like a bailiff. I asked why he was keeping the money himself—it was seven and a half guineas a week altogether—and not giving any of it to the man who was doing the work, even for buying petrol. Do you know what he told me?'

Masters said dryly: 'That he, as incumbent, was legally entitled to the money and in no way bound to pay the lay preachers.'

'Right. Christian-like, wasn't it?'

'Many parsons have treated people like that,' Masters said.

'Maybe they have. But I didn't believe him. I went to see the Rural Dean. Parseloe was legally right and I could do nothing to force him to pay up. I urged him to do so of his own free will. I succeeded in getting him to agree to five shillings a week for petrol. Having done that I resigned. And I think you'll find that with me out of the way he didn't even pay that.'

'I hear lots of things I don't like in my job,' Masters said. 'This is one of them. Have we time for another to wash our mouths out?'

'You were too interested in Arn's story to hear,' Wessel replied. 'Binkhorst called time five minutes ago.'

'We're resident,' Green said.

'But we're not, and I'm a lawyer,' Wessel retorted. 'I don't want to appear in one of your courts on a drinking-after-hours charge.'

'With us present? Be your age,' said Green. 'Can you honestly see Constable Crome bursting in here at the moment?'

Wessel said: 'Come to think of it, I can't. But as I live barely a minute's walk away, would you care to come with me for a nightcap?'

Masters said: 'I've got some writing to do, but if you gentlemen are going to be here tomorrow night . . .?' He turned to de Hooch, who had joined them: 'And you, sir, I shall be very pleased to see you again . . .'

The room cleared very quickly.

Death After Evensong

Masters and Binkhorst were the last two in the bar. The publican came back from bolting the main door. He went behind his counter. There was nothing for him to do. His wife had cleaned up. He stood looking at Masters, who had his back to the dying fire, filling his pipe. Masters said: 'Have a drink with me, landlord?'

Binkhorst said: 'I don't want one. You can have one if you like.'

It was an ungracious reply. Masters wondered what the reason was. He said: 'You'd better join me. Just a short one, because I'd like a word or two with you.'

Binkhorst looked back at him, stolidly. 'Why?'

'Since I hope we'll both be truthful, I'll tell you candidly. I've got the impression that you don't like my being here, but at the same time you'd rather have me here where you can keep an eye on me than anywhere else. So I want to know why. Do you dislike policemen?'

'No more than anybody else.'

'That's a pretty ambiguous answer. Have you ever been in trouble with the police? Been inside?'

'I've never had anything to do with any policeman except the locals when they look in here trying to catch me serving after hours.'

'Have they ever caught you?'

'They couldn't, could they, seeing as I never serve after hours?'

'In that case you've no cause to dislike policemen in general or me in particular. Why don't you want me here?'

'I never said I didn't.'

Masters said: 'Come on, have a whisky. We both know. I can sense these things—hostility, uneasiness, dislike and all the rest. Just as easily as you can tell a drop of good beer.' Binkhorst gave in. He poured two whiskies. They both added water. Masters said: 'Cheers!' and sipped a little. 'Now, where were we? Oh, yes. We were disagreeing. Let's try something else.'

'I can't see we've anything to talk about.'

'We have. A lot. But don't worry about your wife. I'll explain I kept you.'

'There won't be any explaining to do.'

'No? I'd have said she wore the trousers.'

'Would you?'

'Yes. You looked as though she'd told you off tonight for not telling me I definitely couldn't have a meal at half past eight.'

'Oh, in little things, perhaps . . .'

'Not only in little things. What's your religion? C of E?'

Binkhorst nodded.

'And your wife's a Catholic. I'll bet your daughter was brought up Catholic, too.'

'She was as a nipper. But she changed to C of E.'

'Did she? I've never heard of that before. When did she change?'

'When she was about nineteen.'

'Before coming of age? Why did you persuade her to do that? Or are you a keen churchgoer?'

'How can I run a pub and go to church? I haven't been near one for years. I'm in here, Sundays. Dinner time and nights.'

'Then why did you persuade your daughter to change her religion?'

'I didn't. I couldn't have cared less which church she went to.'

Masters sipped his whisky. Then he said: 'That story won't hold water.'

'What won't?'

'I know enough about Catholics to know that the children of mixed marriages are brought up in the Catholic faith. If your daughter tried to change before she came of age, while she was still legally under her mother's care, her mother would have stopped it, unless you, as the father, put your foot down.'

'I tell you I wasn't interested. Her mother did it.'

'So she does wear the trousers.'

'How d'you make that out?'

'She said what had to be done. There must have been some serious reason for it. And yet you say you weren't interested. What was the reason?'

'There wasn't one.'

'I said we'd tell the truth, didn't I? What caused the change of religion?'

'You've no right . . .'

'I've every right to ask what I like. What caused it?'

'Nothing much. All her friends were Church of England. She didn't like being different.'

'Kids don't. But she'd been different for nineteen years. Why the sudden need for change?'

Binkhorst didn't answer. He downed the last of his whisky and rinsed the glass. Masters said: 'It was when she was old enough to have serious boy friends, wasn't it? What happened? Did your wife have her eye on some suitable young chap for Maria? Somebody she thought wouldn't want a mixed marriage? Was that it?'

Binkhorst said: 'Something of the sort. These women all think a lass is on the shelf if she's not married before she's old enough to say her A.B.C.'

'You married your wife when she was only seventeen.'

Binkhorst said: 'Don't I know it.'

'You mean you wish you hadn't?'

'Well—you know how it is. Not like you read about. A man proposing an' all that. These girls, all they want is a ring on their finger. You don't hardly get to know them before they're asking for one. If you can only afford a couple of quid for one they say that'll do fine—till after they're married. Then it's a different business. They want a replacement costing forty quid and an eternity ring and God knows what besides.'

'Are you still trying to tell me your wife doesn't wear the pants? Never mind. What about this young man of Maria's?'

'What about him? I can't even remember his name. He had a bit of brass, I know that. But it never came to nowt. It never does when mothers stick their noses in. Frightens fellers off. And Gina's always been so dead set on getting Maria wed she's tried too hard. Now look at the lass!'

Masters relit his pipe. Then he asked: 'Is she a worry to you?'

'She's not. It's her mother. Making her think that getting wed's the only thing for a girl. That's the Italian side coming out, you know. They're great believers in marriage.'

Masters looked at Binkhorst and said: 'And they're pretty strict about no hanky panky outside marriage, aren't they?'

'That's right. Our Maria never had a chance to put a foot wrong. Not that I wanted her to, but her mother went too far. Acted as a sort of what-d'you-call-it . . . ?'

'Chaperone?'

'Dunt that mean the old bag who was around when a couple of kids were doing a bit of courting?'

Masters nodded.

'Well, our little lass didn't do much courting. So Gina wasn't a chaperone. More of that sort of Spanish spoilsport woman . . .'

'A duenna?'

'That's it. Spaniards and Italians are all the same type, aren't they?'

'They're all Latins, certainly. And incidentally, the Latin word for duenna is domina—a sort of mistress. I told you your wife dominated you.'

Binkhorst said: 'You and me don't talk the same language.'

'Oh yes we do. I'm sorry your daughter's ill. Is it serious?'

'Headache. Flu perhaps. Nothing much. But how did you know?'

'I overheard. What caused it?'

'How the hell should I know?'

'You sounded as if you knew a short time ago. Was Maria out and about rather late last night?'

Binkhorst made a mistake. He started to bluster. 'Here, what are you hinting at?'

'Suggesting nothing. Asking something. Does she always go out on Sunday nights?'

Binkhorst sulked. 'It's one of her nights off. She goes to the pictures.'

'And does going to the pictures usually give her a headache the next night? I think she was somewhere else.'

'Where?'

'I don't know.' Binkhorst's lack of denial had been enough for Masters. He was sure Maria had been running spare—presumably at the time Parseloe had been killed. It was worth noting. Just as a matter of form he said to the landlord: 'And where were you last night?'

'Here, of course.'

'All evening?'

Binkhorst didn't reply.

'I can get to know by questioning other people.'

'All right. Maria goes to the pictures early on Sundays. She's usually back here by soon after nine at the latest. When she didn't get back by half past my missus made me go out and look for her.'

Masters said: 'Did you take your car?'

Binkhorst nodded.

'And did you find her?'

'No. She got back a bit after I left.'

'Where had she been?'

'She wouldn't tell us.'

'I don't blame her, at her age. And where did you go?'

Binkhorst said: 'Nowhere in particular.'

'And what time did you get back?'

'Half past ten.'

'You just drove about, looking for your daughter's mini for an hour?'

'That's right.'

'Go anywhere near Church Walk?'

Binkhorst leaned forward. He said: 'If you're trying to say I done that murder, you're wrong. See?'

Masters said gently: 'I wasn't trying to say anything of the sort. I merely wanted to know if you'd seen anybody or anything in Church Walk.'

Binkhorst said nothing. Again Masters thought the silence told him a lot. He thought a man who had seen nothing would have said so. Suddenly he felt weary. Somewhere a chiming clock sounded midnight. He looked at Binkhorst as though he was going to continue the questions. He thought better of it. Instead, he said: 'What time's breakfast? About half past eight?'

Binkhorst nodded.

Masters said good night.

Binkhorst didn't reply.

As he went upstairs, Masters thought that the omission was a strange one in any mine host. In Binkhorst it might be indicative or significant or . . . he felt too tired to decide.

Chapter Three

Green was bad-tempered at breakfast time. Masters said: 'We didn't have a word together last night. Did you learn anything before I came into the saloon bar?'

'Nothing. I chatted them up, but I might as well have saved my breath to cool my porridge.' It was a reaction against his own failure, and Masters knew it.

'How did the girl look?'

'A bit tired.'

'Not ill?'

'Perhaps she was. She kept well away from me.'

'On purpose? I mean, was she deliberately trying to avoid you? Or is she just a reticent type?'

'Nobody said in my hearing that she wasn't her usual self, so I took it she was acting normally.'

Masters got to his feet. 'I'm going to the station. Meet me there when you're ready.' He went from the dining-room into the tiny hall. He was putting his coat on when Mrs Binkhorst came down the stairs with a young man wearing a duffle coat and carrying a small black case. Mrs Binkhorst was obviously not intending to introduce the newcomer, so Masters said: 'You're carrying a night bag, so I imagine you'll be Dr Peter Barnfelt.'

'That's right.'

Masters introduced himself. Barnfelt was as unlike his father as it was possible for a son to be. Big and fair. The high cheekbones gave a strong look. The hair waved above the ears, giving an impression of photogenic quality. Under the duffle coat he wore a green roll-neck sweater and grey flannels, with fur-lined Chelsea boots in unbrushed pigskin. The hands were so large and capable the night bag appeared to have no weight. The eyes were tired—perhaps worried—and shrewd. Almost wary, Masters thought.

Barnfelt said: 'I'm pleased to have met you, but I'm in a hurry.'

'You've been visiting Miss Binkhorst?'

'I have.'

'How is she?'

'I'm not in the habit of discussing my patients with other people, let alone strangers—and policemen at that.'

Masters stood to one side. He thought here was another one that wasn't overjoyed at his presence. Just for a moment he thought of them as fools for giving away so much so easily. Then he remembered that this was how he learned a lot of what he wanted to know. Barnfelt brushed past him, told Mrs Binkhorst that he would call again and went.

Masters turned to Mrs Binkhorst. 'Has your daughter caught flu? There's a lot of it about, I hear.'

'She has a cold.'

It sounded like an excuse. He said: 'You asked a doctor to call so early in the day for a simple cold? And he's coming back again? You do get good service in Rooksby-le-Soken.'

Mrs Binkhorst looked at him angrily. Her dark eyes glittered. He thought it must be hate. He wondered why. More cause for speculation. He'd never encountered so close a community before. Were they all inimical towards him? The protective herd instinct of the natives? He knew this wasn't true. He'd been treated civilly and openly enough in the saloon bar the night before. Had he, then, been lucky enough to find himself immediately in the midst of the few inhabitants among whom he would find his murderer?

There was no answer he could give himself. He walked the half diagonal across the square from the inn to the police station. Crome was sorting the post. He stood up when Masters went in, and said: 'The Superintendent phoned to say he wouldn't be in Rooksby today, sir. That is, unless you want him for anything.'

'I'd rather have your specialized local knowledge.'

'Mine, sir?' Masters didn't quite know whether the lad was slow on the uptake or overwhelmed by his presence and the prospect of helping the Yard team in some way, however small.

'Yes. Yours. You know most people here, don't you?'

'Yes, sir.'

'Then sit down and tell me about the Parseloe family. I've heard he was a widower with two daughters.'

'That's right. Pamela who's away teaching in Peterborough, but who got back again last night, and Cora who's at home.'

'Cora's the younger one who isn't very bright?'

Crome flushed. 'If you don't mind my saying so, sir, it's a damn shame about her. It's true she isn't very clever and she's not very pretty, but she's not all that daft. The vicar and his wife just made it an excuse to keep her at home in the vicarage and use her as a skivvy. They couldn't get a maid, or couldn't afford one. I don't know which. So they used Cora. She did all the dirty, heavy work and they never let her out. Like a prisoner, she was.'

Masters' opinion of Parseloe, already low, slumped even further. As so often happened in murder cases, he began to feel that whoever had seen off the victim had done the community a favour. He felt Crome was telling him the truth. He asked: 'When did Mrs Parseloe die?'

'About three years ago, sir.'

'What of?'

'Dunno, sir. But she was a skrimpy old besom. Nosy old cat. If you ask me I reckon she died through not feeding herself. A pair of kippers between the three of them for a night time and calling it dinner. That was her sort.'

'And she treated her daughter as a servant?'

'No servant would have put up with her for five minutes. She was worse than old Gobby himself, sir. She had ideas, that one. Tried to be one of the nobs. D'you know, I'll bet they never gave Cora a bean of pocket money.'

Masters said: 'If they never let her out, how do you know all this?'

'It's my patch, sir.' There was a wealth of meaning in this. No further explanation was needed, but Crome went on: 'You couldn't help but notice. That Pamela one was always out flighting around. Of course, Cora did manage to get out now and again, but when I've seen her and spoken to her it was mostly over the vicarage gate. She used to stand there sometimes. Hoping somebody would talk to her, I reckon. Or to see the kids coming out of the old school. Some of 'em were a bit rude to her at times, so I used to make a point of being there sometimes about a quarter to four. You should have seen her hands, sir. You could tell she did all the washing up and dirty chores. A real shame because, as I say, I don't reckon she's half as bad as all that.'

Masters looked at his watch. There was no sign of Green yet. The sergeants had gone to the school to search outside. Masters knew this would be a fruitless task, but it was one he mustn't neglect. Crome broke the silence. 'Would you like a cup of tea, sir, or Nescaff?'

'No, thank you.' He began to fill his pipe. He offered the Warlock Flake to Crome who said he never smoked anything but No. 6's. Masters was thinking back. Something Crome had said was niggling him. It took him several minutes to recall it. Then he said: 'When we were talking about the elder daughter you mentioned that she got back again last night. Who informed her that her father was dead?'

'The Super, sir.'

'And what did you mean when you said she had got back again? Had she been here recently?'

'She only went away on Sunday, sir.'

'She was here for the weekend?'

'For over a fortnight. She came home with a dose of that forty-eight hour flu everybody's been having.'

'And stayed a fortnight recuperating?'

'That's about the strength of it, sir.'

'What time did she go on Sunday?'

'Must have been on the quarter to seven train, sir. There isn't another.'

'But you're not sure of that?'

'I'm not sure, but I saw her at six o'clock near enough, standing with her case at the corner of Church Walk.'

'What sort of a girl is she?'

'Man mad if you ask me, sir.'

'I am asking you.'

'Well, sir, it's no secret. She's not a bad looker, and of course she speaks proper an' that sort of thing, but she's never managed to keep a reg'lar man of her own as far as I know. Her specialty is running other girls off.'

Masters said: 'What on earth does that mean?'

'Well, sir. This Pamela comes home for all those holidays teachers get. And while she's here she gets her eye on some young chap that's already courting, and she grabs him. How she manages it I don't know, but she does. And she don't care what happens. There's been several she's made a fool of. Then of course they've quarrelled with their girls about it, and as soon as that's happened, as like as not my lady Pamela 'ud be back off to Peterborough, leaving the lad high an' dry and the lass down an' wet through crying her eyes out. I've seen it happen a few times.'

'And while she was home on sick leave?'

'She got about a bit. The flu didn't keep her indoors for long.'

'You saw her?'

'Several times. Of course she was here for the Christmas holiday until nearly half-way through January. She'd only been away for about ten days when she was back again. If you ask me she intended it that way. Probably had a bit of unfinished business left over from Christmas.'

'When you saw her, who was she with?'

'D'you know, sir, the funny thing is that every time I've clapped eyes on her since Christmas she was alone. And that's very funny, 'cos it wasn't like her. Not like her at all. It'll make you think I've been giving you a lot of old bull.'

Masters smiled. 'No it won't, lad. It's amazing how often these little oddities crop up. You've helped a lot. And as Inspector Green isn't here yet, I'll have that cup of tea now.'

Green came in five minutes later. He said: 'It must have been that roast pork I ate last night. I was hasty taken. Had to sit there for nearly a quarter of an hour before I dared move.' Masters made no comment. Green had all the ability of the old sweat when it came to demonstrating that he wasn't completely at Masters' beck and call. He showed his independence by resorting to a variety of dodges mighty difficult to disprove. Masters couldn't be bothered to do anything about it.

Green drank a cup of tea noisily, put his cup down and said: 'Now what? Are you going to look for that bullet or projectile or whatever it was?'

Masters said: 'The sergeants are searching the school.'

'That's where we should be.'

'Why?'

'Because we'll never get anywhere until we know what shot him.'

'We'll get round to it. Just at the moment there are several other jobs. First of all, the keys to the school. I'd like to know how many there are, who keeps them, whether the builders locked up properly and so on. I'd like you to tackle that end.'

'What about you?'

'I'm going to the vicarage. After that I'm not quite sure what I'll be doing, but I'll aim to get back here at twelve.'

*

The vicarage garden was neglected. The beds were untidy. The brown stalks of the autumn chrysanthemums and Michaelmas daisies straggled over the unkept grass. Dead leaves sheltered in wind-blown drifts wherever protection was afforded by tree trunks or the edges of the drive. The house itself needed paint. Blotched mossy streaks on the fabric showed where gutters leaked or were blocked. The curtains were drab or sagging. It was an unloved, unlovely home. Masters pressed the bell. He found himself faintly surprised that it worked. He could hear a distant tinkle.

He guessed it was Pamela Parseloe who answered. She was long-legged in nylon tights under a green mini-skirt. At least he guessed they were tights. If they weren't she wouldn't be decent when she sat down. He appreciated the legs. They were firm and well shaped. The green sweater emphasized the figure, small but good. The hair long and dark, slightly wavy. It was the face that didn't appeal. The mouth was petulant, but not full lipped. The nose too short, so that the tip, rather too sharp pointed, was high above the nostrils. The eyes were small but bold. The sort that could be used at will to give a red light or a green one according to mood. The forehead was, surprisingly, well shaped. The voice dictatorial. She said, quite bluntly: 'Who are you?'

He told her, and asked to speak with the two of them. She let him in, as he thought, rather reluctantly. The house was poorly furnished. But in what had been the late vicar's study, a peat fire burned. Masters looked round him. He guessed that the study had doubled as general living-room. There was the debris of communal life around—papers, knitting, books, an open box of Black Magic on the mantelpiece, a grubby coal glove hanging from a fire tidy. The chairs were odd and old, with a few rather brash scatter cushions dotted about. The carpet thin in places. Pamela said: 'As you can see, I'm sorting my father's papers.'

He sympathized with her. He thought she was about twenty-four and whatever her character, her job in the present circumstances was an unpleasant one. He said: 'Is there anything I can do? Or is there an executor to be contacted?'

She replied: 'I can manage, thank you. What was it you wished to speak to me about?'

He said: 'Miss Parseloe, when somebody like your father meets with sudden death, it has to be investigated. And an obvious part of that investigation must be a talk with the closest relatives. I should be grateful if you would kindly sit down, listen, and answer questions.'

She flounced into a chair. It confirmed she was wearing tights.

He said: 'You were here in Rooksby until Sunday evening, I believe. Did you leave by the quarter to seven train?'

'Yes.'

'Thank you. So you were in Peterborough from eight o'clock onwards?'

'Yes. What are you trying to discover?'

'Your whereabouts at the time of your father's death. Could I please have your address in Peterborough?'

'Why? So that you can check up on me?'

'If necessary. We try to be thorough. Elimination is as important a part of detection as anything else.'

She gave the address, unwillingly, he thought. He knew he could have got it from Nicholson, but he wanted the reaction. He was pleased with what he got.

'Now, Miss Parseloe, you left the house just before six, I believe.'

'How do you know that?'

'You were seen. The station is more than a mile from here. How did you get there?'

'By car.'

'Whose car?'

'I don't know. I was given a lift.'

'You'd intended to walk to the station?'

'Yes.'

'With a suitcase?'

She knew she had made a mistake. Her lips pursed angrily. Masters went on: 'The vicar had a car?'

'Yes.'

'Wouldn't he have run you to the station?'

'On a Sunday night?'

'I can't think why not, at six o'clock. His service wasn't until half past. He could quite comfortably have taken you to the Halt and been back here by a quarter past.'

'I didn't ask him.'

He thought that this, at least, had the ring of truth about it. Parseloe, according to reports, might have charged her a taxi fee.

He changed tactics. 'Who were your father's enemies?'

She laughed. It was a harsh, mirthless sound. 'Who wasn't his enemy?'

'You mean he was universally unpopular in Rooksby?'

'That's putting it mildly.'

'Who disliked him more than any of the others?'

'It's difficult to say. He never paid for anything if he could avoid it. He had a devious mind and stooped to the meanest and dirtiest tricks to gain his own ends. He'd do anybody down for money—including me.'

'Why?'

'Because if he'd been a rich man he'd have been a miser. As it was, he could get no higher than this very poor living. So he was practically penniless. And that made him crave for money all the more.'

'But as a parson . . .'

'Parsons are human, just like everybody else. Dad thought people should respect him just because he was the vicar. He didn't realize that respect has to be earned—or bought. And he did neither. He thought traders should be content to wait for their money for a long time—perhaps for ever—if the debtor was the vicar. The people of Rooksby aren't like that. They're hard-headed. Simple serpents fits them admirably. They wouldn't wait for money from Father Peter himself.'

Masters asked if he might smoke. She nodded. He said: 'I understand why your father was unpopular, but you still haven't answered my question. Given me definite names.'

'I don't think I can unless . . . No, no, I'm sure I can't. You must remember I've been away from Rooksby for six and a half years.'

'Unless what?'

'I was going to suggest the ironmonger.'

'Perce?'

'Yes. You know him?'

'We've met. But why Perce?'

'Because we had to have new gates. The old ones were broken and mother insisted on gates that would lock because . . . well, anyhow, she said the gates ought to lock.'

'Because of your sister?'

She was angry. 'You know a lot, don't you?'

'Only what I'm told. But go on, please. Perce and the gates.'

'Mother ordered them from Perce, and then Dad cancelled the order. But Perce had had the gates specially made by then.'

'What caused him to change his mind?'

'When he heard the price—and I can tell you it was little enough for double iron gates—he looked around for some other way of paying. He found one. He heard the Urban District wanted to widen the main road. He offered them three feet off the garden in return for rebuilding the wall and gates. They agreed—as long as Dad agreed they could use the old bricks. He did. Heaven knows what would have happened if the Council hadn't eventually bought the gates from Perce and used them just as mother intended. But I know that Perce vowed vengeance then, and was still doing so as recently as Christmas.'

Masters felt sickened. That a daughter should be able to recount a story like this of her own parents. He wondered whether it could possibly be true. Instinctively he mistrusted Pamela Parseloe. Why should he believe her story? Then he remembered the night before and Jan Wessel's account of the vicar's financial dealings. He said: 'Thank you. Any other person you can think of with a special grudge against your father?'

'Nobody.' She said it with a toss of the head. He knew she'd made up her mind minutes ago. It would be useless to go on. He said: 'I'd like a word with your sister.'

As he expected, she objected. Masters insisted. He followed her through to the kitchen. Cora was washing clothes, using an old dolly tub and wringer. There were none of the modern refinements. Masters wondered how Parseloe had managed to spend what little stipend he did get. According to reports he didn't buy much food; his rates were paid for him, no doubt, as is customary; the house had apparently had nothing new in it since the year dot; and as for Cora's clothes! Even though he was not as expert at women's clothes as he was at men's, nevertheless Masters could tell whether a garment fitted. Cora's fitted—in the places where they touched. It was obvious to Masters that these were her mother's old garments, cobbled to make do for her by an inexpert hand. The colour, material and style were all wrong for a young woman. It would take expert dressing to make the best of Cora's lumpy figure, but at least she could have been given bright colours and young styles. Her sister spoke to her: 'This is a policeman. He's come to speak to you about Dad.'

Cora wiped her hands on a none-too-clean tea towel over the back of a chair, and turned to look at Masters. He thought she must suffer from slight infantilism. No more. He doubted whether she was even severely E.S.N. The eyes were too bright, and though not full of intelligence, showed a kindliness entirely lacking in her sister's. Her hair was a little coarse. He wondered if a regimen of iodine might not do her good. Whether her parents had ever consulted a doctor about her.

She said: 'Please sit down. Can I make you a cup of tea?'

'Thank you, but Constable Crome, the young policeman who sometimes spoke to you at the gate, made me one at the police station.'

'Did he? He's a nice man. I shall be sorry not to see him again.'

'Are you going away?'

'Oh, yes. The new vicar will want this house. I'm washing things so that we can pack them, aren't I, Pam?'

'Don't go on talking,' said Pamela. 'Listen to the policeman.'

Masters neither liked the way she referred to him nor the way she addressed her sister. He said: 'You take your time, Miss Cora. I don't mind waiting. Why don't we all sit down?'

They did so. Pamela with an angry movement. Cora settled herself quite gently, with her hands in her lap. She looked at him steadily. He asked: 'Can you tell me when you last saw your father, Miss Cora?'

'It was at teatime on Sunday. We had toast and Marmite, didn't we, Pam? And a cake. A dripping cake I'd made. It was nice and crumbly. Do you like dripping cake?'

Masters said: 'Is it like lardy cake?'

'Oh, no. It's not greasy like the lardy cake Mrs Longman makes. She's the lady who washes the altar linen and Dad's surplices, and she sometimes brings me lardy cake or sultana buns. She's a very good cook. She comes from Yorkshire. But our dripping cake is like a nice, crumbly sort of rock cake. Very nice. I like it.'

Masters was pleased at her acceptance of him and the way she spoke. He decided she was nothing worse than artless. A natural. Unsophisticated. Not foolish or ignorant. So much better than he had feared, even though Crome—himself an ingenuous person—had recognized and tried to explain that she was simple-hearted more than simple-minded. He felt, rather than saw, that Pamela was tense: alarmed at what Cora might say. It was a pointer that there may be something to hide: substantiation of the fact that Pamela had not told him the truth about her journey to the Halt on Sunday. Or so he felt. And it pleased him that Pamela had to sit by, with ants in her tights, not daring to prompt her sister. Although he would be just as happy if she were to intervene. It would almost certainly give him another lead. He decided to angle for it.

'I must try dripping cake, sometime,' he said. 'Perhaps if you make some more and I'm still in Rooksby you'll remember to save me a piece.'

'I'd like that.'

'Fine. Now, Miss Cora. Did your father go out straight after tea?'

'Pam and Dad went out while I was washing up.'

'Who went first?'

'I don't know.'

'Didn't they come to say goodbye to you?'

'Oh, no. Nobody ever says goodbye to me—except Mrs Longman when she calls. She's nice.'

He turned to Pamela. 'Who left the house first? You or your father?' He sounded brusque. The thought of their lack of courtesy to Cora had riled him. He didn't really care who had left first. But he asked, just the same.

'I think Dad did.'

'Think?'

'I couldn't find him to say I was going. He may have gone over to the church early.'

'More than half an hour before the service was due to start?'

Cora said: 'He always went over ten minutes before.'

Pamela glanced furiously at Cora. Cora didn't notice. She sat watching Masters. Fascinated by him. He guessed there had been few men in her life and there was an animal urge within her to be friendly towards any who were kind. Like Crome and—he supposed—himself.

He said to Pamela: 'Probably you didn't attempt to say goodbye to your father, either.'

She made no reply. He turned back to Cora. 'Weren't you surprised when your father didn't come home after the service?'

'He'd not been coming in straight after Evensong on Sundays for a long time. He usually got in by half past nine.'

'Then you must have been alarmed when he didn't come at all.'

'I wasn't, because I didn't know. I have to get up very early on Sundays to get him up for the early morning service and heat the water for his shave. He liked a cup of tea in bed, as well. So I always went to bed early on Sunday nights to make up for it. I like to listen to "Your Hundred Best Tunes" in bed. Then I go to sleep. Sometimes I heard him come back, but not always.'

'When did you discover he wasn't in the house?'

'Yesterday morning. I saw he hadn't eaten the liver sandwiches I'd left for him.'

'And that's what told you he wasn't here?'

'Oh, no. He always made me leave sandwiches, but he didn't always eat them. I used to fry them for breakfast if he left them.'

'How did you find out he wasn't here?'

'It wasn't for ever so long. He used to like to stay in bed late on Mondays to make up for his hard work on Sundays.' Masters felt sick. He tried not to show his revulsion lest it should alarm Cora and stop the flow of narrative. She went on: 'So I never took his tea up till he shouted for it.'

'Then what?'

'Well, I was washing when a man came to the door. He said he was a policeman, but he was like you. He hadn't got a uniform on. I didn't understand what he was saying.' Masters mentally cursed Nicholson for not having come over himself to break the news gently to this childlike creature.

'What happened?'

'I didn't know what he was talking about. I thought he wanted to see Dad. I tried to send him away because Dad told me I wasn't ever to disturb him in bed. But the policeman wouldn't go, so I went to fetch Dad and he wasn't in his bed. And then the policeman told me he was dead. I was very frightened and he asked me a lot of questions.'

Masters cursed Nicholson anew. Hideous curses. The girl would have been scared stiff at the thought of waking her father in defiance of his orders. He could imagine her trepidation as she went upstairs. The surprise at not finding her father. The shock of the news when it finally penetrated. No wonder she'd been alarmed and unable to answer questions. No wonder Nicholson had said she was a moron and no use to him.

He said gently: 'And that's all you know? You didn't see or hear anything on Sunday which you didn't understand or which was out of the ordinary?'

She looked at him wide-eyed for a moment. He thought she had lost concentration. He realized it was her customary attitude of thought when she said: 'Only the long talk Dad and Pam had on Sunday afternoon.' Masters thought he detected a little sound of annoyance from Pamela. He looked round. She was sitting taut in the kitchen chair. Pressing back as if prepared to spring. He said: 'Surely there's nothing strange in a father and his daughter having a long talk, even if it doesn't happen very often.' He'd kept his eyes on Pamela. As his words showed that he apparently placed little importance in the meeting, she relaxed. Not quickly, but gradually, like a watchdog sinking back after a false alarm. He turned to Cora and smiled, and added: 'Is there?'

She said: 'Oh, yes. It must have been important because Dad always rested on Sunday afternoons. I had to keep the Sunday Express nice for him until then. He always started to read it and then fell asleep. And he was always cross if anybody disturbed him.' She looked straight at Masters and added: 'And they kept me out of the room. I wasn't allowed in to know what they were talking about, so it must have been secrets.'

Masters began slowly to fill his pipe. He asked no questions. Simply looked at Pamela. She stared back for some moments, hot-eyed, and then burst out: 'She's talking silly, dramatic nonsense. I was going back to Peterborough that night and he simply wanted a little talk to ask how I was getting on and if I was planning a move, and things like that. As for keeping Cora out of the room—well, she had some work to do.'

Cora said: 'Ironing your frocks for packing, you said. But I'd done them all in the morning.'

Masters lit his pipe slowly, made sure it was drawing, and got to his feet. He said: 'Well, that explains that. I'm pleased to have met you both and cleared matters up a little. If there's anything I've forgotten, I may have to call again. But I won't trouble you more than I can help, because I know it's pretty distasteful to have policemen always on the doorstep. Don't worry to come to the door. I can see myself out.'

Cora came over and stood close to him. She said: 'Are you going to arrest him now? He's a nice man really, and I was sure he wouldn't do it.'

Masters had to think for a moment. This was unexpected. Unexpected to him and to Pamela, who showed immediate concern. Masters was conscious that the truth could possibly be divulged by this ingenuous girl. He said at last, very gently: 'Who are you talking about?' Pamela was holding her breath. Masters could sense the absolute stillness of her body. Then Cora said: 'Why, Mr Pieters, of course.'

Pamela breathed again. Masters said: 'Why should I arrest Mr Pieters?'

'Because he and Dad nearly had a fight and Mr Pieters said he would get even.'

'When was this?'

'Oh, ever so long ago. Before Christmas.'

'And who is Mr Pieters?'

'He's a carpenter. A nice man. I liked him. He chopped me a lot of firewood when he came, and I didn't have to do it.'

Masters said: 'What was the trouble between your father and Mr Pieters?'

She said simply: 'I don't know.'

He looked towards Pamela. She said: 'Search me. I don't believe I know the man. It must have happened when I wasn't here.'

Masters said to Cora: 'Don't worry about Mr Pieters. I'm not going to arrest him. I might have a talk with him—just to see what the trouble was.'

'I'm so glad. Mr Pieters is a nice man.'

Masters was thoughtful as he walked down the drive. He would have to see Pieters. It was one more to add to the list. He was just about to go through the gate when a Triumph G.T.6 drew up. Peter Barnfelt got out with his bag. He didn't see Masters. Masters said: 'We meet again. Who's the patient this time?'

Barnfelt appeared annoyed at the meeting. He said: 'I thought I made it clear my patients are no concern of yours.'

'But they are—some of them. I want to suggest that when you see Miss Parseloe you consider whether or not she shouldn't have iodine treatment.'

'Miss Parseloe? Iodine treatment? What the hell are you blathering about?'

'Her thyroid must be suspect.'

'Her thyroid's as good as yours.'

'Surely not. Her coarse hair . . .'

'She hasn't got coarse hair.'

Masters said: 'Forgive me. I thought you were about to visit Miss Cora Parseloe. I didn't think that Miss Pamela would be on your list as she lives in Peterborough. My mistake.'

Masters left Barnfelt staring after him. He crossed the road into the school. Hill and Brant were inspecting the other classrooms. Hill said: 'There are loads of prints, Chief. Old ones. Mostly kids'. I reckon the others were teachers'. Nothing outside, either.'

Masters said: 'Try to finish by lunchtime. I'm going back to the station.'

*

After Masters had left him, Green said to Crome: 'Who'd know about the keys to the school?'

'Well, there's Wally Hutson, the verger. He was caretaker of the school as well. Then the vicar would likely have a key himself. And there's Tom Taylor, the builder's foreman. He'd have one, I expect, for getting in and out for the job.'

'Was there a key in the vicar's pocket?'

'I dunno. The Super never said anything to me about the contents of the pockets. But we'll look if you like. They're in the cupboard.'

There was a key of the right type. Green looked at the stamped number and said: 'This looks like a master. Where do I find Wally Hutson?'

Hutson's cottage was one of a row behind the school. Close to a small gate in the church wall, which led along a path to the vestry door. Green found his way there and was told by the woman who answered his knock that her husband was in the church. Hutson was sweeping the flags of the centre aisle. Green noticed that the dust was being swept along to fall through the grating of what had once been the old heating pit. Hutson looked up as he heard Green's footstep clank on the grating, which was half the length of the aisle. He said: 'Who're you? One o' them policemen?'

The verger was tall, lugubrious and slow moving. Green reflected that no other type of man would accept such a job. Hutson was his idea of a time-server—both the way he worked and the state of the church seemed to prove it. Green said: 'Have you got the keys to the school?'

'One. All the rest I gave to Tom Taylor when they started building. One master, front gate padlock, back gate padlock, boiler house, staff room, and four classrooms.'

'And you kept one master.'

'Aye.'

'Why?'

'In case.'

'In case what?'

'In case I ever had to go in, of course.'

Green said: 'Come off it. What would you want to go in for once the school was sold?'

'It wasn't sold. Only let. We're still the owners.'

'Have you been in since the builders started?'

'I haven't been in since we took the desks an' chairs out just after Christmas.'

'You didn't go in this Sunday?'

Hutson leaned on his broom. 'Are you joking? On a Sunday? I don't get chance to call my name my own on Sunday. What with early Communion, Matins, Sunday School and Evensong I hardly have time to eat my dinner.' He spat on the grating and then brushed over it, leaving a smear on the grating.

Green said: 'You're a dirty old devil.'

'Who d'you think you're talking to?'

'You. Anybody who spits anywhere ought to be flogged. In a church it's worse. Where's this key you kept?'

Hutson was surly. He led the way, without a word, to the vestry door in the transept. Here he laid his broom on an old cope chest which even Green could appreciate as beautiful. Hutson said: 'It's hanging on the key board in the robing vestry.' They went up two steps, through the choir vestry lined with cupboards of cassocks and surplices, and into the robing vestry. Here there was a small altar, a harmonium, and heaps of tattered music, all covered in dust. The key board was to the left inside the door. A dozen hooks with a variety of keys. Hutson looked at it. His mouth fell open with surprise. He said: 'It's gone.'

Green said: 'Is this it?' He had the key from the vicar's pocket on his palm.

'Where you get that from?'

'Never mind. Is this the one that's missing?'

Hutson took it. 'Yes it is.'

'How can you tell?'

'By them file marks. I made 'em. People have a happy knack of collaring keys round here.'

'Meaning me?'

'Gobby Parseloe.'

'Didn't he have one of his own?'

'He had one in his desk drawer at home last week.'

'How d'you know?'

'Because Tom Taylor borrowed it. He left his with one of his men who was working overtime to lock up with, and he didn't come in next morning. Tom met me at the gate an' asked me for one. I told him the nearest one was in the vicarage.'

'He managed to get one there?'

'He got in, didn't he?'

'Anybody else have keys?'

'Yeah. There were four masters. The old headmaster, he had one. He didn't hand it in at the end of last term 'cos there was some of his own stuff he had to collect from the staffroom.'

'What's his name?'

'Headmaster's? Baron. He lives in the High Street. House set back a bit near the eight-foot leading up to the mason's yard.'

'He hasn't handed it back?'

'Who hands keys back when they know they're not wanted again? The factory's going to change the locks, else they'd have made sure they got all the keys handed over. And talking of handing over, how about me having my key back?'

Green said: 'You'll have to do without it. It was found in Parseloe's pocket.'

'So he was the one who took it.'

'Looks like it. When did you last see it?'

'For sure? Can't say, but I reckon I'd a'missed it on Sunday morning if it had gone.'

'Why?'

'Because that's when I use all these other keys, see? I open up the choir stalls' book cupboards. The vestment cupboards. West door, East door, the lot. I empties the board except for that key. The choir kids lock everything up again except the doors after Evensong. Right?'

Green said: 'You've convinced me. Carry on spitting.'

Green was a little undecided as to what to do next. He thought perhaps Baron, the headmaster, would be a likely bet, then remembered he would be teaching somewhere else. He decided to locate Tom Taylor. Crome told him where the builder's office was. He was to look for the firm of Coulbeck, near the first crossroads, up the narrow road Perce had emerged from. Green walked fairly sharply. The wind had lessened, but was still strong and cold. It was behind him as he went along the High Street. He turned off into Goose Street. Perce's shop was forty yards up. A flat-fronted shop, wide, shallow, and well stocked. Jonker—Ironmonger and Builders' Merchant. Green stared in. Perce was behind the counter. No customers, no assistants. Green entered. Perce said: 'Come back to say you're sorry, I suppose. Well, you're too late. I know who you are. I've written to Scotland Yard about you.'

Green said: 'That's good.'

'What d'you mean?'

'Well, we keep all the fingerprints at the Yard. They'll take yours off the paper you wrote the letter on. It'll save time later.'

Perce said: 'Don't you try to frighten me.' He picked up a claw-hammer displayed for sale. The handle and head were metal, the grip rubber. Perce's broken fingernails showed up white under the force of his grip.

Green said mildly: 'What's up? Got a guilty conscience? Or are you threatening me? If so, I'll run you in so fast your feet won't touch the ground.'

Perce lowered the hammer. 'You were accusing me of murder.'

'Not yet.'

'Then what did you mean by saying it would save time later?'

'Because it will. I'll get you for something. Maybe not for murder. Now tell me where Coulbeck's office is. Which is what I came in for.'

Perce pointed the way. Green made his enquiries as to where Tom Taylor was working. Coulbeck himself offered to drive him to the place. And because it would have looked daft to refuse such an offer, Green accepted.

Taylor confirmed the verger's story. He'd borrowed the vicar's key on the Wednesday morning to get the men working. The wall hadn't been knocked down by then, so they couldn't start without getting inside for their tools. But he'd collected his own keys from the absent workman's house and then returned the vicar's key before noon.

Green said: 'How did you know the vicar had a key?'

'I didn't. Not until Wally Hutson told me.'

'Who had your keys over the weekend?'

'One of the chippies. A chap called Pieters.'

'Reliable?'

Taylor rubbed his chin. 'I reckon so.'

'But you're not too sure?'

'He's only been with us a few months.'

'But he's a local, isn't he?'

'Yes. He's local all right.'

'So you must have known him for years.'

Taylor looked at Coulbeck. The glance was not lost on Green, who said: 'Come on, now.'

Coulbeck said: 'Harry Pieters is O.K.'

Green said: 'Why leave the keys with a new man?'

'Because he was the one with most tools to leave behind. The brickies just had trowels and spades. Pieters had a full joiner's kit. He was the one most concerned with security, and it was his job to nail up the fence.'

Green could get no more from them. He said: 'I'll see Pieters for myself.' Taylor called the carpenter over. A man of less than medium height. Apparently thin, but with surprisingly big muscles bulging on his bare arms. Dark hair, cut short at the sides, and worn en brosse, holding a few specks of wood flour. The beard area very dark. The eyes brown. Green said: 'You had a key to the school over the weekend.'

'Yes.'

'Where did you keep it?'

'In my trousers' pockets. Why?'

'Somebody got in there on Sunday. Or hadn't you heard?'

'Yes. I heard. And that somebody was Gobby Parseloe. He has a key. Tom Taylor borrowed it last week. He must 'a let himself in and whoever killed him must 'a followed him in. It's as plain as the nose on your face.'

'You know all about it. Perhaps you were there.'

'And perhaps I wasn't. I never stirred out all Sunday.'

'Can you prove it?'

'I don't have to. But you can ask my missus. And the kids if you don't believe her.'

Green said: 'I don't believe in questioning kids. I'll take your word for it that the key never left your house.'

'Of course it didn't. An' if it had done, how'd I have got it back?'

Green looked at him hard. It dawned on Pieters he'd asked a damn silly question. He coloured under Green's gaze, then said: 'I'm not sorry he's dead, but I didn't have nothing to do with it. An' by the piles of Saint Pancras I wouldn't help you to find out who did. I'd more likely shake him by the hand.'

Green said: 'I'd watch my tongue if I were you. It could get you into trouble. I'll likely be seeing you again.'

Coulbeck drove Green back to the office. Green said: 'Didn't anybody like Parseloe?'

Coulbeck had no hesitation in answering. 'If they did, I've not met them. Except a few old women he used to josh along for their money.'

Green walked back from Coulbeck's office. He arrived at the police station as the church struck twelve. Masters was already there, alone in the office.

*

Masters said: 'Any luck with the keys?'

'Does there have to be? There was a key hanging in the church and there was one in Parseloe's house. He could have used either, and he pinched the one from the vestry, which I take to mean he decided to visit the school after he'd left home, but before he left the church.'

'Could be. But somebody else with a key got in besides Parseloe. His key was found in his pocket. He couldn't have locked the door behind his murderer. I want to know if the meeting was by appointment or not, and whether the murderer arrived first or after Parseloe.'

Green sat down and lit a Kensitas. He recounted his morning's work. Masters said: 'I'm interested in this bloke, Pieters. What's he like?'

'Youngish. About thirty. Decent looking. If my opinion's of any value, I'd say he was a good, honest, hard-working man.'

Masters said: 'Don't be so bloody stupid. Your opinion is of great value, and normally I'd take your word for it. But you haven't heard all the story yet. Your decent, hard-working man threatened to do Parseloe in only a month or two ago.'

Green blew smoke through his nostrils. He said: 'I always knew this case was going to turn out a bastard. You'd better tell me.'

When Masters had finished, Green said: 'D'you want me to fetch Pieters in?'

Masters got to his feet. He said: 'It's early days. And bearing in mind your impression of Pieters, we'll just keep him in mind for a bit. What do you say?'

'You're the boss.'

'Meaning what?'

'If I don't fetch Pieters in, what do I do?'

'Go to the vicarage and see if the other key is there. See the headmaster about his key.'

'Why worry about keys? What about the bullet and the weapon? Wouldn't we be better off if we knew how he was killed?'

'We do know. He was shot. Have you ever been worried before about whether a man was shot with a three-eight or a four-five?'

'No. Because I've always known. And I've never met a situation where a bullet never left a mark in plaster or brickwork before, either.'

Masters said: 'Come and have a drink. We'll concentrate on seeing just how many possible or probable suspects there are and then try to cut a few out.'

'We've got a capful of possibles already,' Green said. 'How many more d'you think there'll be?'

'It's difficult to say when a man's as disliked as Parseloe. He had an evil influence over otherwise harmless people. You've just told me about Perce Jonker. What sort of an atmosphere d'you think it has to be to make a half-wit like that lift a hammer to a senior police officer?'

'God knows. Unless Perce was the murderer.'

'Who can tell? But Perce isn't the only one affected. There's Pieters, young Barnfelt, Parseloe's own daughter Pamela, Binkhorst, with his wife and daughter. All acting strangely, to my mind. And we haven't been here twenty-four hours yet. That's why I suggest we should survey the field before placing any bets.'

'We'll have to look at all their teeth.'

'So we will. But some will need closer examination than others.'

They entered the Goblin and hung up their coats. Masters said: 'What'll you have?'

'Seeing as you're paying,' Green replied, 'I'll have a pint of draught Worthington. Nobody offered me a cup of coffee this morning, which shows we're probably as unpopular in Rooksby as Gobby Parseloe was.'

Chapter Four

Green's statement about their unpopularity appeared to be disproved as soon as they entered the saloon bar. Coulbeck and a companion of his own age were there. When he saw Green, Coulbeck said: 'Can I get you gentlemen a drink? Might as well, seeing that Fred Houtstra and I came here especially to see you.'

Green introduced Masters. Coulbeck introduced Houtstra. Binkhorst, looking after both bars himself, fetched the ordered drinks. Coulbeck said: 'Here's health, gentlemen. Make the most of it because you won't see me and Fred drinking together very often.'

Houtstra said: 'That's a fact. Being competitors in business in a friendly, cut-throat sort of way, we don't often team up.'

'You're a builder, too?' Masters asked.

'Same as Dan Coulbeck. Only I'm out of Rooksby a bit. About a mile up the road.'

'I see. And what brought you together today to see us?'

Coulbeck said: 'Harry Pieters. I could see your Inspector was getting a bit suspicious about him. Having the key of the school over the weekend and all that. And Tom Taylor saying we hadn't known him long enough to say whether he was very reliable.'

Masters sipped his gin. He felt a little uneasy. So far the people of Rooksby had appeared clannish, individually. He wondered now whether they were starting to gang up to protect people in whom he or his team showed interest. It seemed so. In his experience, business competitors didn't lightly foregather in the middle of a working day to help the police. Not of their own free will. He said: 'We're naturally interested in who had a key to the school at the time the murder was committed.'

Coulbeck said: 'Of course you are. It's obvious you would be. But Fred and I think we're partly responsible for a bit of trouble that blew up between the vicar and Pieters last autumn. And we thought if you got to hear of that, on top of Harry having the key . . .'

'I had heard something of it. Just a mention. No details.'

'There you are then,' Houtstra said. 'You'll now be thinking the worst of Harry who's a decent, hard-working sort of chap.' Green grinned at Masters over the top of his tankard.

Masters said: 'I'd heard that about Pieters, too. And also that he's a kind sort of man.'

'Anyhow,' said Coulbeck, 'when I saw which way the wind might blow I got on to Fred here, explained the position, and asked him to come along in the hopes of meeting you.'

'Why?'

'Because Fred was Harry's boss before me, and he knows the ins and outs of that trouble between Gobby and Harry as well as I do. In fact, he knows the first half and I know the second.'

Masters said: 'I'd better hear the story.' He picked up the glasses. 'But first it's my turn.' When they were refilled he carried them from the bar and said: 'Suppose we take a corner table . . .'

Houtstra started off.

'Harry Pieters worked for me from the day he left school. Served his apprenticeship, and did good work. He's a joiner, you know, not a cabinet maker. But he's a careful and fast worker if old Dan here hasn't spoilt him with piece work these last few months.'

'Stick to the story—and facts—Ted,' Coulbeck said.

Houtstra said to Masters: 'You'll soon hear how Dan undercut prices. But we were talking about Harry. He's a bit of a singer, you know. Sang tenor in the church choir until this trouble. And that's important to remember. Anyhow, last October, old Gobby was having difficulty in getting anybody to serve as vicar's warden. He'd run through just about everybody who was a possible and they'd all left him, disgusted.' Masters remembered his conversation the night before with Arn Beck and mentally noted that the two accounts were mutually supporting. Houtstra went on: 'So he asked me to take the job on. I wasn't keen. I'd been people's warden for a couple of years way back, and I hadn't got on all that well with Gobby then, so I wouldn't give him a straight yes. Told him I'd think about it. Well, he was a clever devil, or a real bad one. Take your choice. He thought he'd get me to agree by putting a bit of work my way. He asked for an estimate for putting up two or three bookshelves in an alcove. It wasn't worth my time going to look at it really, but I took Harry along as he'd be the one who'd have to do it if we took the job on. I told Gobby it would cost him a tenner. Now what happened next I don't really know, but

I think he realized he hadn't made a big enough impression on me to make me accept his offer of the warden's job. So he thought up a scheme. At the next choir practice he got hold of Harry and asked him how much he'd take for putting up the shelves in his spare time. Because it was the vicar and Harry wanted to do him a good turn, he said six pounds.'

Masters said: 'You're suggesting that the vicar never intended to have Pieters put the shelves up? That his asking was part of a plan to get you to become warden?'

'That's what I think now. But I didn't think so when he rang me up and told me that Harry was undercutting my estimate and pinching my jobs to do in his own time. Now I honestly believe he was doing a bit of creeping with me to get me to accept the warden's post. Showing me what a good chap he was by informing me that my own workman was letting me down. 'Course he didn't tell me that he'd led Harry on, and I was so bloody angry at the time that I sacked Harry on the spot.'

Green grunted. 'Without asking for an explanation?'

'I asked Harry if it was true, and he said it was. If I'd kept him after that every one of my men would have felt free to carry on in the same way. Fair do's all round.'

Green grunted again and waved a hand to attract Binkhorst's attention. Coulbeck said: 'The story's mine from now on. Harry came straight to me for a job and I took him on. Fred had rung Gobby and told him he wouldn't become warden, and so Gobby thought he'd better ask for an estimate from me, because he wasn't going to pay over the odds once he'd lost the chance of Fred becoming warden. Of course I'd heard the story from Harry, so I quoted eight pounds. Old Gobby accepted. I was so disgusted I thought I'd play a bit of a trick on him. I sent Harry to do the job.'

Green choked over his beer. He put his tankard down and looked up. He hadn't seen the tag-line coming. It had caught him unawares, tickling his sense of humour immoderately. Even Masters smiled. 'What happened? Did the vicar refuse to let him in?'

'No. The daughter let him in. The vicar wasn't there but Harry knew exactly what was wanted. He'd been there with Fred, you see. So Harry did the job. Just putting plates either side of the alcove, cutting the shelves, laying them on the plates and beading them. He'd just finished when the vicar came in, and he was a bit shaken to see Harry. Harry left, but the vicar rang me up and said the job had been done badly and wasn't up to specification. I asked Harry about it. He assured me he'd used a bolt-setting tool on the plates as I'd told him, and planed and chamfered the leading edges and so on. As I knew he would. I'd seen enough of his work to know. So I told Harry to come with me when I went to inspect. D'you know old Gobby had been chipping about there with a knife. Said the shelves didn't fit. He was hopping about saying he could have done a better job himself. In the end Harry got a hold of him and said he'd lost one job through the vicar's rotten tricks and he wasn't going to lose another, and if Gobby didn't shut his trap he'd shut it for him and so on. In the end I got Harry away, but I haven't been paid for the job.'

Masters said: 'Did Pieters say he would get even with him?'

'Not to Gobby himself. But he did to me. That simple girl was outside the room when we left and Harry said to me that if it was the last thing he did he'd get even with Gobby. What makes you ask? Did the girl overhear?'

Masters nodded.

Coulbeck said: 'I don't suppose she could help hearing. She put you on to Harry?'

'She told me he'd been kind to her,' Masters said. 'He'd seen her trying to chop some kindling and had done it for her. And she said she was sure he hadn't harmed her father.'

'That's what I think,' Houtstra agreed. 'In the heat of the moment Harry might have bashed him—with good cause. But he wouldn't have laid for him and killed him in cold blood months after.'

'Thank you, gentlemen. I'm pleased to have heard your story.'

Coulbeck said: 'It lets Harry out?'

'By no means. But it casts a much better light on his behaviour. And an equally bad one on Parseloe's. Don't worry. We're not going to hound Pieters or anybody else unless we have very definite and positive proof. Perhaps I'll see him for myself and explain matters to set his mind at rest. I assure you he's got nothing to fear if he's innocent. I know that's easy to say, but we're not out for an arrest at any price.'

Green said: 'Especially not in this case. I wouldn't mind not finding who did Parseloe in. For my money he deserved it.'

*

The sergeants confirmed they'd had a fruitless morning. Masters said: 'And you'll probably have a fruitless afternoon. Inspector Green's tying up the question of keys. I'd like you two to talk to the workmen who were at the school on Friday and again when the body was found on Monday. Who found him? What tools did they leave there? Had any been touched? The lot. A complete picture from their angle. O.K.?'

Green said: 'You still want me to go to the vicarage and the schoolmaster's?'

'Please.'

'What are you going to do?'

'I've got several visits in mind. I want to know what Binkhorst and his daughter were up to separately on Sunday night. I want to see the doctor, and a girl called April Barrett. I shan't manage them all today, but I'll be back by six, I hope.'

Dr Barnfelt senior was not surprised to see Masters. It appeared he was half expecting him. He said: 'That son of mine thinks you're following him around. Are you?'

'If you mean have I bumped into him twice today, the answer is yes. But surely he made it clear that it was he who came to where I was on both occasions, and not the other way about?'

'That's what I told him. You're staying at the Goblin and you had to see the dead man's relatives. In a place the size of Rooksby you can meet the same chap a dozen times a day.'

He showed Masters into the surgery. Barnfelt's eyes twinkled behind his pince-nez. Masters said: 'Your son is very touchy about his patients.'

'No more than he ethically should be, I hope.'

'Perhaps not. I asked him how he'd found Maria Binkhorst and he refused to tell me.'

'Did you really want to know, or were you merely observing the courtesies?'

'Both. Maria was out and about all Sunday evening. Probably half Rooksby was out and about at the same time. But it means I'm interested in her movements and her health.'

Barnfelt said: 'Have I your assurance you are not considering Maria as a murderess?'

'Of course you haven't. I should say it's extremely unlikely that she's implicated, but I haven't ruled anybody out at this stage.'

'In that case, I don't feel at liberty to tell you my son's diagnosis.'

'I don't really expect you to. I had thought perhaps the flu bug or a cold . . .'

Barnfelt shook his head. 'Don't fish,' he said.

'There are several points which I hope you won't regard as deserving ethical reticence. I made a mistake this morning in thinking your son was calling on Cora Parseloe—just to see how she was bearing up under the strain. Evidently he was calling on Pamela.'

'Yes. The elder one was unwell.'

'Was she?'

'You sound doubtful. I have no means of telling—short of asking Peter. But I took an early phone call from Cora. She said her sister had asked her to ring to request a visit from Peter.'

'Is Peter her doctor? She's resident in Peterborough.'

'She's not on his list, but she is his patient—temporarily. He attended her in her recent short illness because she happened to be here in Rooksby.'

Masters said: 'He seems to have all the personable young women on his books. Lucky chap.'

Barnfelt eyed him shrewdly. 'You said there were several points you wished to discuss.'

'Oh, yes. Cora Parseloe. I'd been led to believe she was hopelessly subnormal. I visited her. She answered my questions sensibly enough.'

'Was that why you asked Peter if she should be on a regimen of iodine?'

Masters laughed: 'I'm not much of a doctor, I'm afraid. I just wondered. Thyroid deficiency—iodine.'

'You could be right. I couldn't be sure without examining her.'

'You mean she has never been to see you, or you her?'

'Never. Her parents evidently didn't see fit to demand my services on her behalf.'

'But she is your patient?'

'Yes.'

'Could I ask you to call on her?'

'I can call—merely as a courtesy.'

'Can I suggest to her that she comes to you for an examination?'

'There's nothing to prevent you doing that.'

'I believe that more than half her trouble has been the way her parents treated her. Out in the world she might do something useful and interesting.'

'We can hope so.'

Masters said: 'She'll be alone now, you know. I can't see Pamela saddling herself with a dependent sister.'

Barnfelt looked across at him. 'Was that your real reason for coming? To learn what could be done to help her?'

Masters found himself blushing with embarrassment. 'Well—yes, it was. To ask you to gee-up the welfare authorities. Somebody will have to do something quickly.'

'Leave it to me, Chief Inspector. Believe me, I share your concern.'

Masters said: 'That's a load off my mind.'

'If you're feeling happier, stay and have some tea.'

'What about your son? If I bump into him again he'll really begin to believe I'm dogging his footsteps.'

'Peter has a pre-natal clinic. We'll be undisturbed.'

They went through to the Barnfelts' sitting-room. Mrs Barnfelt, a comfortable-looking woman, was knitting. She said she was delighted to meet Masters and then disappeared to prepare tea. Masters wandered over to the window, overlooking the back garden. He said: 'What's that? A railway track?'

Barnfelt joined him. 'Yes. It's Peter's. He's an ardent railway fan. He builds his own scale models of old steam locos. He put the track up a couple of years ago, but he usually runs his locos at the club track. It's much longer. Right round a large meadow. Gives him a better chance to perform. Lots of intelligent men play at being engine drivers, you know.'

'Why not? But building working scale models must call for a high degree of skill and money.'

'Skill? I should have said interest and application. Peter has never been anything but devoted to medicine ever since he was a little boy. But railways have always been his hobby. And as for money, he regards his hobby as something of an investment. I believe he builds an engine for about three hundred pounds, and can sell it for nearly a thousand. So you see it's not really an expensive pastime, is it? More of a therapy, really. I believe he keeps it up for the rest and relaxation he thinks a doctor should have if he is to do his best for his patients at all times. He's got a small workshop in the basement.' Barnfelt turned to help his wife as she came in with the tray. 'Peter hasn't done much work down there these last few weeks. The flu epidemic has kept him too busy.'

Mrs Barnfelt said complacently: 'And the weather's been against him, dear. It's too wet and windy outside, and the cellar's very cold.' She poured tea from an old-fashioned silver pot. Masters enjoyed himself. He realized time was slipping by, but he felt he couldn't rush away. He hoped

Barnfelt would enlist his wife's help with Cora. Before he left, this had happened. Mrs Barnfelt had said she would see what she could do for the 'poor love'.

Although Masters was feeling happier about Cora as he returned to the police station, there was a niggle at the back of his mind. He couldn't focus it: bring it out into the open to examine it. All he knew was that he felt it to be important. The darkness was coming down and Rooksby looked at its uninviting worst. Much the same as when he had arrived, twenty-four hours earlier. That didn't help his thoughts. In the office he found Constable Vanden, whom he had not met before. He said to him: 'Were you out on Sunday evening?'

'Six to ten, sir. I was a minute or so late, actually. I didn't relieve Constable Crome until just after six at the crossroads. There was a phone call. Lost dog. It held me up.'

Masters took an easy chair. He liked Senior Constable Vanden. His dark hair was cropped so short it showed his scalp strangely white. His full face was brown. The mouth and jaw slightly twisted. The eyes deep set and—Masters thought—sincere. The figure was well made: broad shoulders and slim hips. The uniform was well pressed and the boots highly polished. He carried himself very straight. Masters said: 'Have a chair. I want to talk.'

Vanden sat to attention.

Masters said: 'There were some rum goings on in Rooksby on Sunday evening. And I don't mean the murder.'

'There's rum goings on most nights, sir. But Sunday! It was pretty cold for many of the young 'uns to be up to their tricks in dark corners that night, sir. A few cars about, of course. A few people going to church and chapel early on, but no shennanigan, if you get my meaning, sir. Not that I saw, anyway, and I got round the whole patch.'

'Think back to the cars you saw. In fact, write down every one you can remember seeing—with occupants if possible. Go on. I'll give you ten minutes.'

Vanden went round the table and pulled paper out of a drawer. Masters filled his pipe. Vanden wrote laboriously. The crooked jaw set hard. But he didn't stop until he'd finally finished. He handed the sheet to Masters who refused it. 'Keep it in front of you.' Vanden sat down again, wondering what sort of an exercise this was. Masters continued: 'Now tell me if any of these cars I mention are on your list. Ready?'

Vanden nodded. Masters said: 'Miss Binkhorst's Mini.'

Vanden said: 'Red Mini. Owner Miss Binkhorst. Seen coming in past the new school at approximately six ten. Seen twice later, parked without lights near the junction of Glebe Road and Bowling Lane on site of old pound. Time 8.20 or thereabouts. Owner sitting alone inside, smoking. Again at 9.30 parked with lights just near vicarage gates in Church Lane. Owner in vehicle.' Vanden looked up, tacitly asking for the next question, as if this sort of enquiry went on every afternoon in Rooksby.

Masters said: 'Well done. I've noted that. Now, what about Mr Binkhorst's car?'

'On Sunday night, sir? I didn't see it. Are you sure he was out, sir? It wouldn't be usual.'

'He was out in the last hour of your time on duty.'

'Sorry, sir. He must have slipped along roads where I wasn't. It's very difficult keeping track of everything with just one pair of eyes.'

'I'm not blaming you. In fact, don't bemoan the fact that you didn't see him. Learn from this, lad. It's sometimes nearly as useful not to see—or you should try to make it so. You didn't see him at point A at such and such a time, therefore you know he was somewhere else. You didn't see his car in the village over a period of an hour's patrolling, therefore I'm likely to be right in assuming, for the moment, that he wasn't in the village, but outside it somewhere.'

Vanden perked up visibly. He sat even straighter in his chair. Masters said: 'What about Dr Peter Barnfelt's car?'

Vanden ran his finger down the list. 'You can't miss that one, sir. It's a white Triumph coupé G.T.6. Unsuitable for a doctor, I always think, but just right for a young man like Dr Peter. Handy for carrying the girls about, and they like it. A bit racy, I suppose.'

Masters said: 'You're referring to Miss Barrett, I expect.'

Vanden pursed his lips. 'Used to be, sir. But not lately. In fact, I've seen him with another bird a time or two. A dark one.'

'And Miss Barrett is fair?'

'Real, genuine blonde.'

'Who was the dark girl?'

'Don't know, sir.'

'What d'you mean by that? That the girl was unknown to you? Not one of the village girls?'

'She may have been, and then again she mayn't. What I mean, sir, is that I never saw her face. It's difficult at night to see into one of those little cars through one of those let-down hoods, specially as young Dr Peter usually roars past like a bat out of hell. It's just an impression you get of two people in the car. A head scarf or a smudge of white face.'

Masters said: 'I know.'

'Course, it's different in the summer, sir. With the hood down and the wind blowing the hair away from a girl's face. You get a good view then.'

Masters said: 'But in spite of it being winter now, you're pretty sure it wasn't April Barrett?'

'Absolutely, sir. I'll swear it was a dark girl, not a blonde. And I've seen the car go past with this girl in it and seen the Barrett girl standing on the pavement looking after it. An' if you asked me, sir, I'd say she didn't like it.'

'You mean April Barrett used to come into Rooksby to see what Dr Barnfelt was up to?'

'I'm not saying that, sir. All I know is I've seen her standing around the village a bit more these last few weeks than I ever saw her before. An' she was never with Dr Peter. For long enough before that I never saw her without him. I reckon they've had a bust up, those two.'

Masters thought for a few moments and then said: 'Where did you most often see Miss Barrett standing?'

'Sometimes at the crossroads.'

'Near the Co-op?'

'That's right, sir. Two or three times there, and once or twice at the end of Perry Lane.'

'Where's that?'

'You wouldn't know, sir, but there's an electric sub station . . .'

'I remember. That's not far from the doctor's house.'

'Quite right, sir. You can't see the front of the house from there, but you can see down the ramp into the doctor's garage.'

'Then it does look as though Miss Barrett was keeping an eye on her young man, doesn't it?'

'She must have got it bad, sir.'

'I suppose so. But let's not waste any more time on April Barrett. Where did you see young Barnfelt's Triumph?'

'Coming in from the south just after eight, sir.'

'From the Peterborough way?'

'That's right. Then I saw it on the garage ramp at the house half an hour later. It wasn't run into the garage.'

'That was all?'

'Well, sir, I didn't actually see it again, but I heard it about ten minutes after that. I can tell its note, if you know what I mean, sir. He's added twin big-bore copper tail pipes and lord knows what else, so that it's unmistakable round here.'

'Which way did he go?'

'North, I think, sir. I reckon I heard him back out on to the road and then shoot off along Hunters' Crescent. That curves round into the main road a hundred yards along. If he'd wanted to come south he'd have come towards me.'

Masters said thoughtfully: 'I see.'

'I know it sounds a bit of a muddle, sir, but . . .'

'No, no. It's fine. Any idea where he could have been going?'

'To a case, I reckon, sir.'

'He was off duty on Sunday night.'

'Then I dunno, sir. But there's a roadhouse that's a favourite with him about four miles out, side slip off the new bypass. He's often there, I hear. I could ask about Sunday, if you like.'

Masters thought for a moment and then told Vanden not to make enquiries at the roadhouse. But he asked for its name—the Nutmeg Tree.

*

Green visited the vicarage. He grimaced at the sight of it. Cora let him in. He asked for Pamela. She had gone out without letting her sister know where she was going. He said to Cora: 'Did the vicar have a key to the school?'

'Did nice Mr Masters send you?'

He gulped back an angry retort. 'Yes.'

'Then I can tell you. He used to keep it in the middle drawer of the desk, but it's not there now.'

'You're sure?'

'You can come in and look.'

She showed him into the study. He was by her side when she pulled open the drawer. The key was there, lying apart from the other articles, which had been tidied up. Paper clips, old ball-points, rubber bands and adhesive tape. All tidy. The key sitting alone. Cora said: 'That's funny. It wasn't there this morning. I tidied this drawer to help Pam. I told her it wasn't here and asked her if she'd got it and she said no. She must have found it later.'

Green said: 'That's about the size of it. Do you mind if I take it?' Before she could answer he picked it up. 'Well, Miss Parseloe, I won't keep you. I expect you're having lots of callers today.'

'Oh, no.'

'No?'

'Only Mr Masters and Dr Barnfelt to see Pam. And you, of course.'

'I see. P'raps it's just as well you're not being kept too busy answering the door. Tidying up's hard work. So I'll say goodbye.'

Green was thoughtful. He'd objected to this key lark, but even he had to admit that Masters didn't often get fanciful ideas. The verger's key had been taken. Now it appeared that the vicar's key had at any rate been mislaid. Perhaps that was why the vicar had taken the verger's key. But it was unlikely that his own could have gone far astray in the two or three days since the builders had borrowed it. He wondered how this knowledge would help. He was still wondering when, following the directions given him by Hutson in the morning, he reached Baron's house. He found it easily enough. One of the few houses in the High Street with a front garden, alongside which ran the eight-foot leading to the open gates of the mason's yard. Chunks of marble and granite, grey, white, black and red: 'In Remembrance' pots squatting under lids perforated to hold flowers: a few curbed gravestones lined with marble chips. Green wondered what it was like to live so near to the outward reminders of death. He supposed people got used to it. He didn't think he would.

A woman of about forty-five opened the door. She was plump and fair, with large, pale blue eyes and a smile that Green appreciated. She smiled at him even before she spoke. He wondered why, and then realized she probably smiled at everybody. She was that sort. He thought every headmaster would be wise to pick one like her. She had an apron on. Green liked it because it was not the usual rectangular sort, but a frilly affair, triangular, with the apex at the top. Clean and crisp. Like the white blouse under the blue cardigan. Her legs and feet were neat. Green thought she was quite a dish—the best he'd seen in Rooksby to date. He said: 'I'm Detective Inspector Green. I wonder if I could see Mr Baron?'

She said: 'He's not back from school yet. But I'm expecting him any time after four. Would you like to wait?'

He followed her in. There was a smell of smoked haddock cooking. He guessed it was for Baron's tea. Green sniffed appreciatively. He liked smoked fillets, kippers and bloaters. Thought them some of God's better inventions. Thought Mrs Baron must be a good wife to cater so tastily for her husband's appetite. She showed him into the sitting-room of the front-middle-and-back and switched on a convector. She said: 'I expect it's about the vicar?'

Green said: 'I'm checking up on keys to the school. I understand your husband has one.'

She said: 'There now! If I've asked him to return that key once, I've asked him a dozen times. But would he do it? No. Always the same excuse. He could never see Hutson.'

'Why Hutson? Why not the vicar?'

'Jim wouldn't have returned a brass farthing to the vicar these last six months.'

'Oh? Why not?'

She seemed to realize she'd said more than enough. Appeared anxious to get him out of the house. 'Is it just the key you want?'

He nodded.

'I'll get it for you.'

She was away for some minutes and then returned. He thought she looked more bedworthy than ever when flustered. 'It's not there.'

'Where?'

'In the little drawer in the dressing-table. It's been there ever since Christmas.'

'Perhaps your husband moved it.'

'I've looked everywhere. It's gone.' She saw the gravity of his heavy features. She said: 'Oh, my God. What does this mean?'

'Probably nothing. Let's hope so. But remember a murderer got into the school and somehow managed to unlock and lock a classroom door without doing any damage.'

'You mean he had a key.' It was a quiet, despairing statement. Green nodded. She asked: 'How many keys were there?'

'Three other masters. The builders, Hutson and the vicar each had one besides your husband. Now don't get upset. There may be a simple explanation for its disappearance.'

She sighed, and sat down opposite him. He noticed she sat with her knees and feet neatly together. She clasped her hands in her lap. 'I do wish Jim would hurry up.'

Green offered her a Kensitas: lit them both. He said: 'Don't let the fish burn, will you?'

'It's cooking very slowly. Oh, I'm forgetting. Perhaps you'd like a cup of tea.' She left him before he could reply. He liked the memory of her back view, too. He'd always thought of headmasters' wives as nosy old bags. Now he was altering his opinion. She was back inside two minutes with a butler's tray which he opened and set up for her. He stood so close to her he could smell the faint fresh odour of baby soap. He'd never believed grown women used it. But this baby did. And very nice, too, he thought.

The tea was strong. He liked it like that. He'd had two cups before Jim Baron's key was heard in the door. She called: 'In here, darling.' He came in with a handful of books: dropped them in a chair. She said: 'This is Inspector Green, Jim. He's come for your key to the school, but I can't find it.'

He kissed her and said: 'I've got it here.' He took it from his jacket pocket. Green studied him. Balding slightly, with a dark widow's peak. Clear grey eyes. Slight jowls, giving an ugly strength to a jaw already faintly stubbled. Dark sports jacket and trousers. Blue shirt. Brown shoes. Hands clean and well manicured with a whiteness of chalk dust round the cuticles. Green said: 'Why are you carrying it with you?'

'To return it to Hutson, the verger.'

'When?'

'If I'd seen him I'd have given it to him today.'

'You've had it for a couple of months. Why take it out today?'

His wife handed Baron a cup of tea. She smiled nervously.

'I thought I'd better give it back, and then decided to keep it.'

'Why?'

He set down the cup and lit a cigarette. 'In view of what happened in the school on Sunday night. I'm not a fool. I knew the police would make enquiries about the keys.'

'And your first thought was to get rid of yours?'

'Yes.'

'But on second thoughts you decided to hang on to it. Why? Because you thought it would look fishy, off-loading so soon after the event?'

'Something like that.'

'Why don't you tell me why you and the vicar didn't get on these last few months?'

Mrs Baron said: 'Oh, that's not fair. You asked me . . .'

'Don't worry, ma'am. I'm not here to trap your husband. But somebody got hold of a key to the school on Sunday.'

'The vicar had one himself,' Baron said. 'Couldn't he have let the murderer in?'

'He could have. But the murderer couldn't have locked the door behind him, leaving the vicar's key in his cassock pocket, could he?'

'Oh, my God. Tell him your key was still here, Jim.'

'It was. In the dressing-table drawer.'

Green said: 'Fair enough. Now tell me why it was there and not returned as it should have been.'

'Pure laziness on my part. Nothing more.'

'But you weren't very friendly with the vicar.'

'Tell him, Jim. Don't make a mystery of it. Tell him about the rotten way you were treated.'

'There's no reason why I should keep quiet,' Baron said. 'You'll be able to check what I say. You know I was headmaster of the Church School until it closed down at Christmas?'

'Yes.'

'Parseloe, as vicar, was chairman of the management committee. Three years ago, when his wife died, he decided he'd have his elder daughter, Pamela, come back to Rooksby to teach, and to keep house for him. Privately I thought it was so that she could bear most of the financial burden. But that's beside the point. He came to me and said he was arranging to have her appointed to my staff. I'd already got a full complement. I was satisfied with their work, and as far as I knew none of them was contemplating leaving me. I told Parseloe there was no room for his daughter. He suggested that I should engineer a vacancy.'

'Engineer? You mean make a bad report to the Management Committee about one of the teachers so that she would get the push?'

'That's right. Parseloe had already told Pamela he wanted her back in Rooksby. That didn't fit in with her plans. She didn't want to come. She preferred a freer life in Peterborough. So she'd already been to me and asked me not to find a place for her. I'd no intention of doing so, because Pamela was not my cup of tea. I'd rather have been a member of the staff short than have her in the school. She has a bit of a reputation, you know, in Rooksby.'

Green nodded.

Baron went on: 'So I reassured her, and when he came, told her father I'd have nothing to do with his scheme. Told him it was the sort of game I wouldn't be party to, and that if he attempted to interfere with my staff in any way I'd have the N.U.T. on to him before he could say "let us proceed in peace".'

'What happened?'

'I heard no more about it. Then, last summer, the staff for the new Comprehensive was appointed. I'd applied for the headship, and as the sitting tenant, was fairly sure of getting it. But because the new school was replacing the Church School, the vicar had been appointed to the new Management Committee. When the appointment of the headmaster was discussed, Parseloe opposed my application. And he carried the day. The Committee was not made up of locals, otherwise it might have been different. They came from as wide a catchment area as the school serves, and they didn't know Parseloe. And when the man you've worked for for umpteen years says he's dissatisfied with you—says, among other things, that you're unco-operative, it doesn't do your chances much good. I didn't get the job.'

'How d'you know he did you dirt?'

'I was told. There's not the slightest doubt it's true.'

'Then what?'

'I was going to be out of a job at Christmas. I got a post as assistant head at the village school in Towton. Took the place of a man who had been lucky enough to be appointed to the new Comprehensive.' Baron sounded bitter. Green could understand why. Wondered if this example of Parseloe's particular brand of Christianity had led to murder.

He asked: 'Where's Towton?'

'Five miles east of here. It's an easy run in the car along a secondary road. I leave myself a quarter of an hour for the journey.'

Green got to his feet. He said: 'I'll keep the key.'

*

All four of them met in Masters' room at the Goblin. It was six o'clock and dark outside. Inside the lights were on, the curtains drawn, the room was warm, and out in the corridor was the good smell of sage and onion farce cooking inside the duckling Mrs Binkhorst was preparing for dinner.

Masters and Green brought each other up to date. Then Sergeant Hill said: 'We've seen the workmen. Four of them. Pieters the joiner and his labourer; Smith the brickie and his paddy.'

'Get anything out of them?'

'Well, Chief, they're a pretty dumb crowd. They'd been working there a week. Each night they'd used that same classroom for locking up their tools. The brickie didn't have anything of much value—trowels, a couple of hammers, plumb, level—that sort of thing. Pieters had much more. One of these portable electric saws with all its bits and pieces besides a bag of valuable planes, a bolt setting tool, hand saws, brace and bits—the lot. It was a haul worth having, but evidently it was too heavy for toting to and fro on a bicycle. So they left it locked up on the site. I asked them if they didn't think it could be pinched. They said they didn't think so. So I asked them if anybody knew it would be there over the weekend, and they just said they supposed everybody in Rooksby who thought about it would know.'

'Had they lost anything at all during the week—not just at the weekend?'

'Nothing. Of course we couldn't check, but that's what they said.'

'Were they telling the truth?'

'I think so.'

'Were they worried?'

'A bit. You see they've got hold of several stories. One says somebody got into the school and the vicar saw whoever it was going in or saw a light shining and went in to see what was going on.'

'Somebody who'd gone in to pick up what he could find?'

'That's the point, Chief. They're equally torn between the idea that a thief went in on spec and that he went in on purpose to pick up their tools. If it's the second they're feeling sorry for themselves. Think they were the indirect cause of the murder.'

Masters lit his pipe. Brant, sharing the edge of the bed with Hill, said: 'And as for seeing anything, you'd think they're all blind.'

'In what way?'

'I asked 'em all separately to describe how the body was lying and got four entirely different stories. I know we don't expect all stories to tally exactly, but this! Over a simple matter of how a body was stretched out.'

Masters said: 'Who found it?'

Brant said: 'Pieters. He had the key. Two of them were already waiting when he arrived. The fourth came a minute or two later. After the others had opened the classroom. They all agreed they'd got right into the room before Smith noticed the body.'

'Pieters leading?'

'He opened up and led the way in.'

'What about the boards nailed over the hole in the wall?'

'Some of them had been moved. They said they thought kids had broken in for a lark.'

'They weren't worried?'

'Not a bit, apparently. They said kids break in everywhere these days.'

'Did they touch anything in the classroom?'

'They said not. Pieters told them to leave everything as it was and sent his labourer for P.C. Crome. They stood around outside until Superintendent Nicholson told them they could take their tools to another job.'

'Is that all?'

'That's the lot, sir.'

'Right. Well you've just time to jump in the car, drive out to the Nutmeg Tree, which you'll get to just before you reach the by-pass, and make some enquiries about Dr Peter Barnfelt.'

Green said: 'You're considering him, then?'

'I've got to. He was scudding around Rooksby footloose on Sunday evening. You told me the vicar's key reappeared during the day, and he was the only caller at the vicarage other than ourselves. It is possible he brought the key back, because Pamela Plum-Bum was definitely not ill when I was there this morning, although that was the excuse for his visit.'

'I get you. I'd had something like that at the back of my own mind.'

'What d'you want to know?' Brant asked.

'Whether Peter Barnfelt was there on Sunday evening. If so, times and occurrences. Don't be obvious. He already suspects I'm chasing him. Diplomacy—casual acquaintance role—recommended to call by the doctor etcetera, etcetera. And don't stay long. Be back here for dinner.'

'I'm not missing that duck for anything,' Hill said.

The sergeants left. Masters walked over to the washbasin. Green lit a Kensitas and said: 'I don't like it. Not knowing the weapon, I mean. When are we going to get round to sorting that out?'

'Why don't you have a bash at it?' Masters said.

Green thought this was typical. Whenever an insoluble part of a problem came up for discussion, he was asked to have a go. Keys, weapons, projectiles. That was the sort of thing he was always told off to investigate. Masters just sat around and talked. And then got the kudos. He said: 'So you agree it's important?'

'Obviously.'

'I began to think you were prepared to ignore little trifles like weapons.'

Masters dried his hands. 'No. I try not to ignore anything. And with you around to keep reminding me, I rarely do. Got any ideas about the gun?'

'None.'

'Then you'll be starting cold, won't you? And that's what we'd all have been doing if we'd concentrated on it from the start.'

'You're talking as if we'd already got somewhere.'

Masters said mildly: 'I think we have. For one thing we've established that nearly everybody we've spoken to had a grudge against Parseloe at one time or another. So we've got a few suspects. Four or five. That's not bad going in twenty-four hours, is it?'

Green stubbed his cigarette. 'As long as you're satisfied,' he said. 'When are we going to sort them out?'

Masters straightened his tie. He thought this was how Green always reacted. Grumbling. Masters wondered whether Green had sufficient mental equipment to see far enough through a plethora of facts and hints ever to come to any sort of conclusion, satisfactory or otherwise. He said: 'Unless I'm mistaken, we'll not have heard the last of the grudges against Parseloe. We can't really start to pick a winner till we've studied the form of all the runners.'

Chapter Five

It was Masters' first view of Maria Binkhorst. The sergeants had returned to say that Peter Barnfelt had been in the Nutmeg Tree from about nine o'clock on Sunday night until half past ten when the bar closed. He had been alone and had drunk steadily. Which was evidently unusual for him. The barman had heard he'd had a row with Miss Barrett, who usually accompanied him to the roadhouse, and put his solitary drinking down to an effort to drown the sorrows of a lovers' quarrel. Masters was satisfied with the report. He was even more satisfied to find Maria waiting on them at table.

'Is this your mother's night off?'

'She's in the saloon bar,' Maria replied. 'Dad didn't think I was well enough to be in there from half past five till half past ten. So Mum took over.'

'And gave us the exclusive pleasure of your company. We're definitely lucky. But we were sorry to hear you were ill.'

'It's . . . nothing.'

'We're pleased you're up and about again.'

She placed tureens on the table. Inviting, pale green crockery, white lined, that showed up baby carrots and peas to advantage. The duckling she brought on whole. No rice. No orange slices. Plain cooking. Masters said: 'Fit for a king. I'll carve.' He turned to Maria. 'D'you want any of this back?' She shook her head. 'Good.'

She held the plates for him as he carved. He had a chance to sum her up. As Hill had said, she was slender. But the Italian early maturity was there. She was a woman, not a girl. Dark-haired, pale complexion, with dark eyes very alive. Her lips were strangely full, but not petulant. Masters seemed to remember they were what his mother used to call 'bee-stung'. They had an inviting smoothness that stirred memory for him. Her figure was lithe. He supposed the real term was sinuous. As he carved the breast of the duckling his thoughts were not on the job. He was thinking that Maria knew how to dress, too. He guessed her skirt was less than eighteen inches long. Her legs, not too heavily thighed, erotically shapely. He was sorry when she'd handed round the plates and left. He ate in silence, thinking about her. To him she had none of the external signs or symptoms of a girl who is unwell.

Green ate voraciously. He called for beer with his meal. Masters took no liquor. He preferred to savour the food. Even so he was not really aware of what he ate. Hill and Brant kept quiet. They were used to Masters tacit at some stage in every enquiry. Suddenly he looked across at them and said: 'When you saw the workmen, was one of them injured? Bandaged?'

Brant nearly choked. Hill said: 'How did you know that?'

'I didn't. I asked.'

'Sorry. Pieter's labourer had a chisel cut on his left thumb. A big bandage, stained yellow.'

'Acriflavine?'

'I wouldn't know.'

'Orange-yellow. Antiseptic. Germicide. Wound disinfectant?'

'That sounds like it.'

'When did he get it?'

Hill said: 'I asked him. He said last Thursday morning. They had to get the doctor to him.'

Masters said: 'To him? They didn't take him to the surgery?'

'They definitely said "to him". I can remember being a bit surprised. Then I thought that in a place this size the doctors probably find it easier and quicker to go out in their cars rather than have injured people trying to cycle in or wait for an ambulance to come from a long distance.'

Masters said: 'Thanks. They didn't say which doctor answered the call?'

Hill shook his head. Masters said: 'Not to worry,' and lapsed into silence again. Green grimaced and got on with his meal. Maria came in again. Masters said: 'Have you had your supper?'

She answered unconcernedly: 'We have high tea before opening time and then another snack after we're closed.'

'Nothing in between?'

'Not usually, but I had a couple of the sausages tonight. I kept them back from the ones I did with the duckling.'

'Because you're going to bed early tonight as well?'

She pouted. 'No. I'm going to watch television. Then I'll get Mum and Dad theirs.'

He grinned. 'And some more for yourself?'

She reddened and took his plate. He asked her no further questions. Hill was looking at him closely. Green and Brant were paying no attention. He got up from the table. He said to Green: 'Would you and Brant care to take the spit-and-sawdust for half an hour? There are a couple of old blowhards in there who might be useful. Harold and Matthew. They hinted there might be things to learn about various characters around here. But they're cagey. See what you can do to draw them out.'

Green said: 'You've met them already. Wouldn't it be better if you saw them again?'

'Sorry. I told Wessel, Beck and company I'd see them in the saloon. But don't worry. It's the same beer on both sides. And if you have no luck, come and join us. One other thing. Binkhorst seems uneasy. Keep your eye on him and let me know your impression of what's eating him.'

'Guilty conscience?'

'Could be. He was cavorting around on Sunday night when he should have been behind his bar.'

Green grunted and went out of the dining-room with Brant at his heels. Masters and Hill passed through to the saloon.

As soon as Masters entered the bar he was called over to a corner table by Wessel. 'Mr Masters, this is Jim Baron. He tells me he was visited by Inspector Green earlier today, and would like to meet you.'

Masters said jovially: 'And I him. How d'you do, Mr Baron. Did you come along specially, or is this your usual place of call?'

Baron said: 'I drop in most nights.'

'Not last night.'

'Never on Mondays or Thursdays. I teach at night-school now. Income lower since I lost my headship. So I'm making up with a bit of overtime.'

'What do you teach?'

'Mathematics on Mondays, woodwork on Thursdays.'

'Quite a mixture.'

'Maths is my normal subject, but woodwork's my specialty. You know. We have to study some non-academic subject like music, P.T., metalwork, drama or something akin at college to make us more desirable as teachers in the eyes of school management committees. There was a vacancy for a woodwork man, so I took it. Unless you do two nights a week it's not worth doing any—financially.'

Masters accepted a drink brought over by Arn Beck. Masters thanked him and then turned back to Baron. 'I'll ask the obvious. What time did you get here on Sunday evening?'

'I didn't. Not on Sunday.'

'Churchgoer?'

'At one time. Not in the last few months.'

Baron didn't attempt to expand his statement. Masters didn't press him. It was neither the time nor the place for close interrogation. He said to Beck: 'Does Farmer Barrett ever come in here?'

'Phil Barrett? He used to come in most nights, but I haven't seen him for—let me see—ten days or a fortnight. Want to pump him too?'

Masters said: 'Pump? No, I don't think so. Unless he has something significant he wants to tell me. I was hoping to buy a sack of potatoes from him.'

Wessel said: 'And we can believe that or not as the fit takes us, I suppose?'

Masters nodded. 'You certainly can. And if you come to any good conclusions let me know. I'll be interested.'

'Case as bad as that? Floundering a bit, eh?'

Masters smiled. 'I don't think so. And you can believe that or not as the fit takes you, too.'

Beck said: 'You've a reputation.'

'For truth?'

'For successful investigation.'

'Thank you. Does it worry you?'

Beck's eyes twinkled. 'If I said yes, you'd arrest me. And if I said no you'd call me an irresponsible citizen.'

Masters laughed again. 'Sorry. I can't help trying to score points.'

Wessel said: 'You mentioned last night that you'd like to see us here this evening. Any particular reason?'

'Just one. I want to know why Maria Binkhorst is not married. I think it would be embarrassing to ask the girl herself. Her mother has already told me she can't understand why her daughter is still single. Her father? He seems totally uninterested. So I'm asking you. You're men of the world. You've probably watched her grow up. What's the reason for her being on the shelf?'

Baron said: 'Is it any business of yours?'

Masters looked at him squarely. Thought he sounded like one of those permissive tutors who regard the police as Establishment bullies. 'I think so. Just as your hanging on to a school key is my business in the present circumstances. If the information about Maria is of no help to me, I shall forget it soon enough. Just as I'll forget you have—or had—a strong motive against the vicar, kept a key, and haven't accounted for your actions on Sunday evening.'

Baron flushed. 'Are you accusing me of murder?'

'If I were, you wouldn't be here. All I'm pointing out to you—as vividly and personally as possible—is that some sort of case could be made out against many innocent parties. My job is to find the guilty party. Nothing more. But to do it—to make absolutely sure—I have to poke my nose into lots of private holes and corners. In the interests of justice. And at this particular moment I want to learn more about Maria. Shall I tell you why? She was driving round Rooksby on Sunday evening, and her father, too. Now, according to my information, Maria often goes out on a Sunday—but always to the pictures. Because of this, her father never reckons to leave the bar on Sundays. These are just two odd facts I have nosed out. In fairness to everybody—including yourself—who may be implicated in the case, I must try to find an explanation for these unusual happenings. Now, when I hear of a young and personable girl trundling around in the dark, I immediately think she's involved—perfectly innocently—with a man. If I hear her father has chased her, I suspect it's because he knows and doesn't approve of the man in question. But I must try to make sure I'm right. The easiest way is to ask somebody what the girl's reactions to men are. If she hates them like poison, then I'm probably off net in thinking she went out to meet one.' He spread his hands. 'I could go on like this for hours. What I ask is my business, Mr Baron, and it's probably in the girl's best interests, too. I like to think so.'

Baron looked shamefaced. 'I'm sorry. I hadn't looked at the problem from your point of view.'

Masters, thanking heaven Baron had swallowed his story, said mildly: 'Why should you? I wouldn't understand the philosophy of teaching a child to read.'

'So Binkhorst and Maria are under suspicion?' Beck said.

'In so far as they're not accounted for on Sunday evening. So's Mr Baron. So are you, until you're cleared. There are two thousand possible suspects in Rooksby alone. Naturally we rule out children and elderly women—at first—unless we've reason to think otherwise. But why should I suspect Mr Baron more than Joe Bloggs? I mustn't. I can't. Until I know Joe Bloggs is innocent. And the easiest way of proving any man innocent is to prove another guilty. Sorry, but that's the way it is in a case like this where the victim seems to have been everyman's enemy.'

Masters was beginning to get tired of explanations. He tried not to show it. He had deliberately suggested this meeting so that he could gather informed gossip. Use it to get the atmosphere of Rooksby and its inhabitants. The milieu, the ambience of a crime always helped him. The customers in the public bar had their value, but they were more clannish. More mistrustful of outners. They would give just so much away, then no more. He wanted these people to talk.

Baron said: 'I taught Maria.'

'A Catholic in a C of E school. Did she feel out of it?'

'I was only a young teacher at the time—not the headmaster—but we tried to make sure she didn't.'

'But she did a bit?'

'It was inevitable. We had more than our fair share of Parseloe's visits.'

'Was she a good girl? Well behaved?'

'Extremely. We saw to that in school, and mama saw to it outside.'

'A bit of a dragon?'

'No. Nothing like that. But she made a fool of the kid. Always had her so well dressed she was frightened of getting dirty or tearing her clothes. And Gina toted her around. Took her on shopping expeditions instead of letting her play with the other kids.'

Wessel said: 'Gina was scared stiff some undesirable character would get her.'

Masters said: 'I understand you have an unenviable reputation for early, shot-gun marriages here in Rooksby.'

Beck said: 'All these little isolated communities have. And if you were to trace the histories of the inhabitants you'd find practically everybody is related to everybody else. Why there aren't more batties born in Rooksby beats me.'

Masters said: 'Promiscuity and fecundity seem to take the place of inbred weaknesses. No wonder Mrs Binkhorst worked hard to keep her daughter clear of trouble. She succeeded, too.'

Baron said: 'She packed Maria off to a Convent School when she was eleven. Travelled every day by bus from the market place here.'

'Was she a clever girl?'

'So, so. She got one or two O levels. Not academic ones. Her mother insisted on cultivating the wifely virtues, Italian style. Sewing, cooking—that sort of thing.'

'She certainly cooked a damn fine dinner tonight.'

'Then, when she left school, she came straight into the pub. I thought at the time that it was a bit of a waste, but her mother could see nothing wrong in it. And she wanted to keep her eye on the girl.'

'She must have attracted some boy friends. She's a looker.'

'Of course she did. One in particular. Jeremy somebody or other . . .'

'Pratt,' said Beck. 'I remember the first time he saw her. He was passing through and stopped for a drink. Sports car, good clothes, plenty of money. He came in here, and he saw Maria. They were both teenagers and fell flat for each other. Needless to say, mother encouraged it.'

'To the point of allowing her to renounce her religion and change to C of E?'

'That's right. You do get to hear things, don't you? It gives you some idea of how keen Gina was on the match. She thought they were going to get married, all right.'

'What went wrong?'

'Old Pratt. Self-made man. Lord knows what he bought and sold to make his brass, but he was determined Jeremy shouldn't marry Maria.'

'Does he live close by?'

'Near Spalding. At first he thought he'd scotched things by saying he didn't want Catholic grandchildren. Then when Gina allowed Maria to change, he had to think again. Or rather, he gave his real reasons for objecting. He said he wouldn't allow his son to marry a barmaid. He must have brought some powerful pressure to bear on Jeremy, because the affair finished all of a sudden.'

'With what effect on Maria?'

Baron said: 'I'm pretty sure it's affected her ever since. She was really in love, you see. Not available to be caught on the rebound like so many little lasses whose emotions don't really get involved in their affairs of the heart.'

'She steered completely clear of men friends?'

'For the most part. She attracted them, but either she wasn't keen or Gina wasn't. In a place like this word soon gets round. The local lads aren't good enough for Gina. Those that are don't stay in Rooksby to marry Maria.'

'So Maria at twenty-eight is left high and dry, and mother wonders why.'

Wessel said: 'Wonders? She's nearly crackers about it. Wants like hell to see her married—suitably. D'you know, it's only about six months ago—you remember, Arn—old Gobby was here and . . .' Masters interrupted. 'Parseloe used to come in here?'

Beck said: 'Occasionally. Just in time to join in a buckshee last round with no chance of standing his own corner.'

Masters grinned. 'Thanks for the hint.' He looked at Hill. 'Would you mind?' He handed over a pound note. Hill got up immediately. He realized Masters didn't want Mrs Binkhorst to come to the table at this juncture. Her appearance might stop the flow of gossip at just the wrong moment.

Masters said to Wessel: 'Please go on. Parseloe was here . . .'

'Oh, yes. Gobby made some remark to Gina about Maria. Asked if she was out courting because she wasn't serving. That was an example of Gobby's sense of humour. It was one of Maria's nights off, actually, but trust Gobby to put his foot in it. Gina must have been feeling very confidential or it might be that she had an inbred respect for the cloth—of whatever denomination. Anyhow, she told Gobby, with two or three of us standing round, that she couldn't understand why no man of standing regarded Maria as a suitable catch, considering she was heiress to the Goblin—which is a free house—and already had a dowry of over two thousand pounds.' Wessel took his drink from Hill, and continued: 'Those are the lengths Gina's gone to. The old Italian idea of saddling a girl with a dowry. If that isn't asking for trouble, I don't know what is. But you'd know more about that, Chief Inspector. Ageing spinsters with a bit of money. They're natural prey, aren't they?'

Masters nodded. 'There have been cases—Brides in the Bath types. But I would hardly call Maria ageing.'

Beck said: 'In Rooksby, an unmarried girl of twenty-eight is already aged. Remember we have grandmothers here of thirty-two or a bit over.'

Masters suddenly felt sick of the whole business. Weary. In every case the time came when unsavoury details momentarily caused emotion to overcome reason. This time the plight of a girl—comfortably housed, with more than enough of every material benefit to make life bearable—inextricably hemmed in by a maze of parochial and parental barriers, roused anger in him. Momentarily. He'd heard enough from these new-found acquaintances. Enough about Maria at any rate, for the moment. He switched the conversation perfunctorily.

'I like your doctors. Or should I say I like Dr Frank Barnfelt? I've had no chance of getting to know the young one.'

Baron said, very seriously: 'I think Dr Frank Barnfelt is the most brilliant, capable and practical man I've ever met. And I've met a few—at college and so on.'

Masters asked: 'As a doctor?'

'As anything. His doctoring's only one facet. He's the sort of chap that could have followed any profession and made a success of it. He only happened to choose medicine because his father was a doctor. But the odd thing is he's without any ambition on his own behalf. If he had that to drive him on he'd be unstoppable. D'you know, he reads both Latin and Greek for pleasure!'

Wessel said: 'And he knows more about the law than I do. Where he gets it from, I can't imagine. How he has time to read and imbibe material that an ordinary family lawyer would boggle at is totally beyond me. He's put me right several times. Given me an argument for court that's enabled me to win hands down on two or three occasions.'

Masters was interested. More interested than he'd expected to be. He'd formed the opinion for himself that Barnfelt was something more than just a run-of-the-mill G.P. His discourse on bruising had been authoritative. He said: 'Does he write? Medical stuff, I mean?'

Baron said: 'I've not heard that he ever produces medical papers, but he's written a cookery book emphasizing the proper use of protein. He came down hard on the side of bully-beef, I remember, And he publishes original plans for steam locomotives . . .'

Masters said: 'I thought locomotives were Peter's hobby.'

'They are. Inherited, though. Dr Frank built him his first working steam engine when he was two.'

'With his own hands?'

'Entirely by himself. He's a remarkable man. And a funny one.'

'Funny?'

Beck said: 'Are you talking about his clothes and his squeaky voice?'

'No. He is a much cleverer man than Peter in every way, but he's so proud of that boy you'd think the positions were reversed. D'you know what I think? It's my honest belief that old Frank never really believed he could father a son. And when he managed it he was lost in awe at his own prowess.'

Wessel said: 'Come off it!'

'I mean it. I think he thought that for some reason—known only to himself, and based on some genetic theory of his own—that he half expected to be unable to sire a family.'

'You mean he diagnosed himself as . . . what? A hermaphrodite? Not a complete male? Because he had a peculiar voice and an odd choice in clothes?'

'I don't know. But I can think of no other reason for him being so proud of Peter.'

'I'll grant you he's proud of his son. Thinks the sun shines out of his backside, even. But many fathers do the same. It's quite natural, and fairly common.'

Baron stuck to his guns. 'I still think he's too fiercely proud for it to be natural in a man as intelligent as he is.'

Masters said: 'There's nowt as queer as fowks.' What else he was about to say was lost as Green came up and said: 'D'you know what I've just learned?'

'What?'

Green sounded disgusted. 'That to be really good, onions should be pickled for seven years. Like whisky.'

Masters knew Green well enough to realize that his colleague had spent a fruitless evening in the public bar. This was his way of saying so in public. If Green ever got hold of anything worthwhile he always bottled it up until a moment of climax. His appearance now signalled the break up of the party. Binkhorst was due to call time at any moment.

Masters drew Green on one side. 'I'd like to talk to all three Binkhorsts. After the pub's cleared.'

'D'you want me with you?'

'Please. Arrange it as gently as possible. While they're eating supper, if they don't mind. As long as it's tonight.'

The Binkhorsts' living-room was ornate, but pleasant. There was a predominance of burgundy in the colour scheme. The upholstery plush. The photo frames gilded. The fireplace old-fashioned, with highly polished copper reflector plates and figured register. The table had an intricate lace cloth, beautifully laundered. The dishes were leaf green. The cutlery silver. Masters wondered whether Binkhorst had ever become fully attuned to living in the midst of a decor that smacked more of southern Italy than the east Midlands of England. Gina looked fully at home. Maria, too. But Masters was worried about all three. Binkhorst was sullen— and not just because he had company for supper. Gina and Maria were apprehensive. Or so he thought. He didn't like it. He felt it would militate against frankness and he wanted the truth above all else at this time.

Maria carried in a pizza, round and red and hot. She slid it off the glove oven-cloth on to a wrought iron table guard, and went back to the kitchen. When she reappeared she was carrying a tub jar of prawns. Her mother offered her a plate of pizza. She said: 'Not for me, Mom.' Her mother stared at the prawns for a moment and then snatched them away. She said, angrily: 'They are not good for you now . . .' and then bit off her words, turning to glance fearfully at Masters.

Masters smiled at her and said: 'I don't know a lot about it, but I think I agree. Pickled prawns in the first trimester would seem to me to be unwise.'

His words induced a silence, tangible, hard, complete. The room and the people in it resembled Tussauds. Everybody frozen in mid act. Green burnt his finger on a flaring match. His oath broke the silence. Maria said: 'He knows.' Relief. Even Binkhorst, as he put his knife and fork down, seemed to sink more comfortably in his chair.

'Now let's talk this over sensibly. I've no wish to pry into family secrets. Please remember that Inspector Green and I are very discreet, but we must know certain facts if we are to stop prying into your affairs. And I believe that telling us the truth will help you as much as it will us.'

Gina said: 'It is a disgrace. She is a bad girl.'

'Perhaps. From one point of view. But I'm not concerned with moral issues of that sort. More with cause and effect.'

Binkhorst pushed his plate away. 'I'm with you there. I'm not sure that this is all Maria's fault, though she's carrying the can.'

Green said: 'That's one way of putting it. And I hope you're not going to let her down.'

Gina flounced round in her chair. 'You do not know. It is terrible this thing she has done.' The girl got up and put her arm round her mother's shoulders. Gina started to weep, sobbing, 'She must be married to have babies. It is not right to have babies without marriage.'

'It's not all that bad, Mom.' She looked across at her father. 'Is it, Dad?'

'No, love. Don't mind your mother. She's a bit upset. So am I if it comes to that. But she'll see us through. You can bet your life on it.' The girl gave him a quick smile of gratitude, kissed her mother and sat down.

Masters was pleased at Binkhorst's attitude. Previously he had thought him a henpecked nonentity. Now he appeared to be taking a grip. Just at the time when there was crisis. Masters thought how often the hour calls forth the man. Green said: 'Don't you think it would be an idea to let them—and me—know how you knew.'

'Bits and pieces. Like a doctor calling early in the morning. As Maria was well enough to be up and about later it must have been a very temporary indisposition—not flu, or a nervous breakdown or anything serious. And when girls are sick in the morning one immediately jumps to obvious conclusions. Her eating habits at the moment—three suppers in one night. That immediately makes one think of the old wives' tale of eating for two. The craving for pickled prawns—or similar unsuitable foods—is, I believe, sometimes a feature of pregnancy. And so on.'

Green flung his cigarette stub on the fire. Binkhorst said: 'You're a clever bastard, aren't you?'

'It doesn't matter. Everybody will know soon enough.' Maria didn't sound despondent. Rather happy, in fact. Masters was surprised. He wondered why she should be happy. He said: 'So now we come to what interests me most. Your movements on Sunday night.'

Gina turned to him. Her eyes red-rimmed. A tigress. 'They didn't kill him. They should have. I should have. But they didn't.'

Masters said soothingly: 'That's just what I think. But I must make sure. So can we clear the whole matter up now and then forget it? Remember, Mrs Binkhorst, that worry at this time won't help your daughter.'

'Worry? It is all worry. I am worried. How can we not be worried?'

Green said: 'Who's the father?' It was said unconcernedly. A blow with a blunt instrument. Gina started to weep again, noisily. 'Now what have I said?' he asked.

Masters said: 'I believe—correct me if I'm wrong—that the late vicar was the father. Am I right?'

Maria nodded. Green swore. 'The dirty old . . . well, I'm damned. By God I've heard of some things, but this takes the biscuit.'

Masters said: 'I know that for some time past the vicar has not been returning straight home after Evensong on Sundays, as he used to. Sunday is also one of Maria's nights off. That seemed significant to me, particularly when I heard that Mrs Binkhorst had told the vicar that Maria had a considerable dowry and other expectations.'

Gina let out a wail. Her husband said: 'So you opened your mouth to old Gobby, did you?' He went on reproachfully: 'You should have known better, lass. I bet he swallowed it like a donkey taking strawberries.'

'He did,' Masters said. 'It's not very complimentary to your daughter, but I imagine he started paying attention to her from that time on.'

Maria said: 'In September.' It was a quiet, pitiful little reply. Her father reached over and took her hand, clumsily but kindly meant. 'I'll never know how you came to let him, lass. But I'm not blaming you.'

Masters said to him: 'How long have you known?'

'Her mother guessed a week ago but said nothing to either of us,' Binkhorst replied.

'Until when?'

'She told me on Sunday night she thought our Maria was pregnant.'

'Did she also tell you who she thought the father was?'

'I didn't know that until Monday. Gina didn't, either. It wasn't until after we'd heard Gobby was dead. Maria fainted when she heard. That's when we got it out of her.'

'You're sure?'

'Course I am. Otherwise I'd probably have got him before the other bloke. And I hope you don't catch him. He's done me a good turn, whoever he is. And a lot of others.'

Masters said: 'Right. So now there's no difficulty about explaining what you were so reluctant to tell me last night.'

'There's no mystery.'

'Not for you, perhaps. But I've been put to the trouble of tracing Maria's movements. What I found out led me to the conclusions I've already given you. She left here ostensibly to go to the pictures. She came back to Rooksby in her car shortly after six. Was that to see Parseloe on his way over to the church for Evensong?'

'Yes.' She whispered it.

'You were a little late, weren't you? He set out from the vicarage before six.'

'Did he?' There was genuine surprise in Maria's voice.

'Had you an arrangement?'

'For a quarter past.'

'Where?'

'In the lane near the vestry gate.'

'That's the one that runs between the school and the churchyard?'

'Yes. Nobody uses it after dark in winter.'

Masters was thinking hard. From what he had learned of him, Parseloe was not the one to miss an appointment which was to his own advantage, without very good reason. This thought opened up many avenues. 'Forgive me, but a meeting at a quarter past six would leave you very little time together.'

'It was only for making arrangements for later.'

'I see.'

He didn't. Not quite. But if Parseloe had dodged the meeting at a quarter past six, it might have been because he wanted to avoid the later one without having to give explanations. In which case, he may have already planned to meet somebody else instead. In the school. This meant that the rendezvous with his murderer could have been prearranged. The thought interested Masters greatly. A meeting Parseloe had not wanted to mention to Maria! The vicar was a devious type—the sort who would duck one meeting to avoid giving reasons for ducking another. Bent as a hairpin. He'd go to any lengths to avoid telling an unpleasant truth face to face. He said to Maria: 'After missing him before the service you then waited for him at the old pound?'

'I thought he would come there.'

'Because that was where you usually met?'

'Yes. It was quiet. Close to the church. And I could sit in the car off the road.'

'What happened?'

'You already know it all, don't you?' It was a reproach.

He said: 'I'm trying to find it all out. When did you move to Church Walk?'

'About nine o'clock.'

'Why?'

'Because he hadn't come to the old pound.'

'But why the vicarage gates? Did you go to the door?'

'No. Oh, no. I waited to meet him coming home. I thought he might have been called out—to see somebody sick or dying. The flu. Lots of people have been really ill.'

'And the vicar was consequently very busy. I understand.' He turned to Binkhorst. 'Why did you go out?'

'To look for Maria, of course.'

'Why? She usually went out on Sunday nights.'

'Maybe she did. But she'd never been pregnant before as far as I knew. When her mother told me how she was I put my coat on and went.'

Masters smiled. 'To look for the man?'

Binkhorst growled: 'What the hell d'you expect? I didn't know who it was, but I wanted to find out.'

'And?'

'How the hell could I know it was old Gobby? I thought it was . . . somebody else.'

'Jeremy Pratt, for instance?'

Binkhorst's face was laughable in its incredulity. Maria said: 'Oh, Dad.'

Binkhorst grumbled: 'You're a bloody good guesser.'

'Sometimes. So you went haring off towards Spalding? What did you do when you got there?'

'Nothing. Old Pratt's gates were locked. Iron ones. I couldn't get in. I waited a bit and then came back. Maria was home by then.'

Masters got to his feet and knocked out his pipe at the fireplace. He said: 'Well, that seems to have cleared matters up a little. You see how sensible and easy it is not to try to hide things at a time like this.'

'We didn't want you to know,' Gina said. 'It is the family disgrace. It has nothing to do with your murder. Nothing.'

Masters said quietly: 'I'm sorry, Mrs Binkhorst. I thought it had. I still think so.'

'How can it be? We have done nothing to your Gobby.'

'But he has done something to you.' Gina burst into tears again. 'And what he did and whom he did it to almost certainly have a bearing on his death.'

'Well, at least you won't go on thinking it was Dad. You might as well suspect me of killing him.'

Masters said enigmatically: 'Quite.'

She said accusingly: 'You do think it was me.'

Green said: 'You were in Church Walk. You knew him pretty well and he'd done you dirt. What d'you expect?'

Masters silently cursed Green for his intervention. Nothing he could say now would calm them. Gina was weeping. Maria was staring. Binkhorst was on his feet. Masters said: 'That's quite correct. But it's not as bad as it sounds. Remember we haven't even gone so far as to search the Goblin for a weapon or anything of that sort. So you see we're not too suspicious of you. However, there's a long way to go yet, and you're not out of the wood. But I think you've gone a long way towards clearing yourselves tonight. If I can confirm what you've told me, you'll be all right. And don't worry about Inspector Green and myself knowing your secrets. We won't let them out.'

They left without another word from the Binkhorsts. When they were out of the living-room Green said: 'You're not taking their word for it, are you? If you do you're more easily satisfied than I am.'

'I thought you'd have understood that I already knew the facts. All they did was confirm them for me.'

'It strikes me we're getting nowhere fast. I knew we were going to be snowed under with suspects. Now we've got so many on the hook you're beginning to throw them back into the water. That's not the way I fish.'

'Nor me. I'm putting them back in the water—in a keep net. I can haul them out again to be weighed when the scales come round. Meantime I don't want to harm them.'

'So on top of everything else you're an angler, too.'

Masters said angrily: 'Oh, for God's sake, man. We've got to take a chance sometimes. You want me to get bogged down and flounder about here until the cows come home. I'm not going to. I'm going to bust this case wide open before the weekend.'

'O.K. I'm happy. Rooksby's not my idea of a holiday camp. But there's no need to take it out on me when the going gets tough.'

'Who says it's tough?'

Green stared. 'I suppose you already know the answer.' It was a sneer. Masters looked at him squarely. 'I didn't say that. But I don't consider it tough. Just mucky. As ditted up as Charlie M'Clure's waistcoat. Eggfilth.' Masters went up the stairs. He'd had enough of Green for one day. Was sorry he'd asked him to stay for this late-night session with the Binkhorst family.

Chapter Six

By Wednesday morning the wind had gone down. A pale sun gave Rooksby a lick and a promise of better things to come. As Masters breakfasted he wondered what effect it would have upon the communal psyche of the inhabitants. He said to Green: 'What about the weapon?'

Green was reading The Sun and crunching cornflakes. 'Are you asking me? I've been harping on it ever since we got here.'

'So you have. But last night you said you'd give it your undivided attention today.'

'If that's what you want.'

'I do want.'

'With no leads to give?'

Masters said: 'With no leads other than those you've already got. Take Brant. See what you can do.'

'What about you?'

'Barrett's farm. With Hill.'

'For a sack of spuds?'

'Among other things. They'll ride home in the boot.'

'Not with all the clobber we've got, they won't. There's hardly room already.'

Masters got up. 'I've a feeling things will work out just fine. You'll see.' He left the dining-room. Green said to the sergeants: 'He's worse than ever. Woman crazy, if you ask me. First the girl in the nick. Then there's this Italian bint—just because she's infantizing he's acting like a midwife. And there's that Cora one—the one that's only elevenpence ha'penny to the shilling. He's more concerned with getting her some treatment than he is in finding out who did her old man in.'

Hill said: 'It's not a bad way to be. If you can manage it all at the same time as doing a good job of work. Some of us can't, of course.'

'If that's a crack at me, watch it. We're here to find a murderer, not wet nurse a crowd of Boers. When we start getting paid for welfare work's the time to start feeling sorry for people.'

Hill said: 'I can feel sorry for some people all the time.' He got up and followed Masters. Green said to Brant: 'Your oppo's getting sassy. If you want to do him a favour, warn him.'

Brant put his napkin on the table. He said: 'He's had a tough time lately. You know that as well as anybody. I'm not going to make it tougher. What about this weapon? Where do we start?'

Green said: 'You are a considerate man, aren't you? Would you please give me your considered opinion about the weapon?'

'Haven't a clue.'

'That's a lot of bloody help.'

*

Hill drove Masters along the flat roads bathed in watery sunshine. The daffodils that had survived the wind stood up bravely in front gardens. The grass sparkled and stood up as if planted in sponge. The water, still high in the drains, had a surface tension that gave Masters the same impression as cheap sun glass lenses. Dirty grey-green, hiding lord-knows-what.

Hill said: 'Tough is it, Chief?'

Masters grinned. 'As tough as Billy Whitlam's bulldog. Every case is.' He remembered denying this to Green the night before, and added: 'Though I wouldn't admit that to everybody.'

Hill could guess who.

There was a silence for about a minute. Then Hill said: 'Funny thing. I switched on our radio this morning, just to make sure it was working, and found we're nearly bang on net with the local cops.'

Masters said: 'I shouldn't have thought so. We're all supposed to have distinct wavelengths. Probably because The Soke's so far from the smoke they thought they could safely allot us both the same band.' He flicked on the radio. There was no traffic on the net. He looked across at Hill. 'Seems all clear now.'

Hill said: 'That's odd. I distinctly heard a request for an ambulance. Didn't take much notice as it seemed pretty routine and I was only on just long enough to make sure we were working. Ah, well! A reception freak, I suppose.'

Masters filled his pipe. Noted that the tin of Warlock Flake was nearly empty and didn't reply. The niggle at the back of his mind had reasserted itself. He couldn't clarify it. The sight of Barrett's farm drove it from his mind altogether. The car stopped on a dry cobbled apron.

Hill said: 'That shed's the office. Or do you want the house?'

Masters chose the office. A blonde in her early twenties was working at the desk. She said: 'Can I help you?'

Masters guessed this was April Barrett. She was wearing a roll neck sweater, slacks and gumboots. But there the resemblance to a landgirl stopped. Her pale gold hair was styled in an expensively simple way. The make-up emphasized its quality by being barely perceptible. The nail polish was not outrageous. The fingers not workworn. The eyes very big and blue—Masters privately dubbed them bedroom eyes—and the mouth generous and well-shaped. He could feel Hill's interest in her. Altogether an attractive girl. He said: 'I am Detective Chief Inspector Masters, and this is Sergeant Hill. I would like to speak to Mr Barrett, please, if he's available.'

'Father's out somewhere. I'm April Barrett. Is there anything I can do?'

Masters half sat on the corner of the desk. He said: 'Miss Barrett? I've heard of you.' He saw the startled look in her eyes. 'Oh, nothing bad, Just casually. In the course of conversations during my investigation.'

'The vicar?'

'Yes. A miserable business.'

He thought she looked unhappy. It might be of use to him. 'And I've met your fiancé, Dr Peter Barnfelt.'

She said sharply: 'He's not my fiancé.'

Masters was at his smoothest. 'I beg your pardon. I must have been misinformed or picked up the wrong story. But I'm certain I heard your name linked with that of Dr Peter. But there, I've heard so much about the inhabitants of Rooksby these last two days I probably can't tell t'other from which.'

She looked straight at him. 'Peter and I used to be very friendly.'

'Not any more? I'm sorry. I've probably put my foot in it. Please forgive me.'

'There's nothing to forgive.' She sounded miserable. 'It's not your fault. It's . . .'

'Whose?' Masters spoke quietly. 'Whose fault? A dark-haired girl's? A girl who can't be identified through the side curtains of a Triumph coupé?'

She was angry now. 'Mind your own business.'

'This is my business. Let me give you a bit of advice and help.'

'I don't need help.'

'Maybe you don't. But probably Peter does.'

She said bitterly: 'He can look after himself.'

'That's just my point. He can't. He's been got at.'

Now she was scornful. 'Got at? You don't know what you're talking about.'

'Oh, but I do. For instance, I know that you think Peter has recently been keeping company with Maria Binkhorst.'

She stared incredulously.

Masters nodded. 'Maria's a pretty girl. With long dark hair. The only one in Rooksby that you thought could possibly be attractive to Peter.'

'You can't possibly know what I think.'

'I can. You've told your father so.'

'So you've already spoken to Daddy?'

'No. But I know he hasn't been to the Goblin for a fortnight. Before that he was a regular. What caused him to stop? I think the reason for his disaffection is a desire to have as little to do as possible with the Binkhorsts. Particularly Maria, of whom he may be quite fond—through long association in the saloon bar.'

'And you say it wasn't Maria?'

'It wasn't. Honestly.'

'Who was it then?'

'Somebody you'll never believe possible. Pamela Parseloe.'

She gasped in surprise. 'That cat? With Peter?'

'It surprises you? It shouldn't. You think she's such an abominable creature that no decent man would have anything to do with her. But that's not quite how it goes. She's got something attractive to men—for a time, at any rate. Remember her reputation for taking other girls' boyfriends? After a time they get scared of her and back out. She's too predatory. That's why she can't keep one for herself. But she manages to hook them temporarily.'

'That's what you meant when you said Peter was in need of help?'

'Your help. To get out of her clutches.'

'I did think it was Maria. It never entered my head it could possibly be . . . that woman.'

'Well, now you know.'

'Yes. Thank you. You said Peter needs help . . .'

'He does. Lots of the right sort. You see, he's made a fool of himself. But you're not the girl I think you are if you need me to tell you what to do.'

She blushed. 'I'll ring the house and see if Mummy knows where Daddy is.'

'Please don't bother.'

'You don't want to see him after all?'

'You can pass the message on. He can go back to the Goblin now with a clear conscience. The only other thing was, I wondered if I could buy a bag of King Edwards'.'

She laughed. He understood. Pure bathos. He wanted it that way. To remove the tension. She said: 'I'm sure you can have one. There are a few in the filling shed.'

They collected the bag from beside the sizing belt. Hill carried it to the car. April refused payment, but as she said goodbye reminded Masters that he had promised her some advice. He looked at her gravely, liking what he saw. She had brightened up. Out in the open, her hair shone—rivalling the sunlight. Her shoulders were straighter, emphasizing a figure that even a sloppy-joe sweater could not diminish. He wondered how Peter Barnfelt could ever have discarded this girl for Pamela Parseloe. He felt it confirmed his opinion that Pamela had offered much in the way of inducement. 'Just one little piece of advice. Never play bridge again.'

She looked astonished and coloured under his gaze. He guessed she had misread him. Thought he was referring to the mistaken call that had caused the open rift between herself and Peter. He didn't elaborate. Hill had already started the car.

*

The niggle at the back of his mind. Masters found it there again on the way home. He gave it full rein. With no luck. Hill pulled up behind a white Triumph G.T.6 coupé in front of the Goblin. 'It looks as though the doctor is visiting Maria again.' Masters got out and walked forward. Because the sun was out, Peter Barnfelt had lowered his hood. Masters noted the twin big-bore tail pipes: copper blued by exhaust heat. Looked inside the cockpit. A dashboard full of instruments and a supplementary switch panel installed above the hump of the transmission housing. Black toggles, two inches long, banked neatly and skilfully. Hill said: 'He's souped this up. He's got everything. Vacuum gauge, parking light, car compass, twin flasher unit . . .'

He was interrupted. 'Looking for something?' Peter Barnfelt had come out of the front door of the Goblin. Hill said: 'Admiring it, you mean. I could do with a job like this myself.' Peter Barnfelt didn't reply. He stepped over the door into the driving seat. Then he said, offensively: 'They're for sale in all the dealers'. They might even give you a leaflet if you were to ask nicely.' Hill's face flushed and his hands clenched. The doctor started up. Revved unnecessarily hard: a mechanical raspberry, petrol flavoured. Went away with too much accelerator, so that the back wheels spun before gripping the road. Burnt rubber smell on top of exhaust gas. Hill said: 'The miserable bastard. And that's the chap we went out of our way to do a good turn to this morning.'

Masters grinned. Hill, glowering, wondered why. He was pretty sure Masters wouldn't grin at his discomfiture. Unexpectedly Masters said: 'What's the time?'

'Half eleven.'

'Right. Come on. To the station.'

Hill kept pace. He said nothing. But this was Masters cheerful. More cheerful than he'd been for months. His face was lifted to the sun, his pipe cocked up at an angle between his teeth. He took the steps up to the office at a run—light and lithe, two steps at a time. Vanden jumped to his feet. Masters said: 'Take a pew and tell me everything you know about young Dr Barnfelt's car.'

'How d'you mean, sir?'

'It's got everything but the kitchen sink.'

'Yes.'

'But no car radio that I could see. That's funny, isn't it?'

Vanden smiled crookedly. 'Not really, sir. There's no room. He's got a two-way radio for urgent calls when he's away from the surgery.'

Masters smiled. 'That's what I thought it had to be.' He turned to Hill. 'That's the answer to your pick-up this morning. I'll bet the Barnfelts' frequency is very close to ours, and whichever one of them was asking for an ambulance this morning would be so nearby that you picked him up loud and slightly distorted—by induction.'

'Could be. They do interfere when they're sited close to each other.'

Vanden said: 'I'm sorry if they were a nuisance, sir. I could get H.Q. to check their frequency allotment.'

'Don't worry. Have you heard from Superintendent Nicholson?'

'He'll be in this afternoon, sir. The inquest's at two thirty in the Parish Hall.'

Masters got to his feet. 'I shan't be there. But if the Superintendent wants me I'll be around Rooksby somewhere.'

'Right, sir.'

Hill followed Masters down the stairs. Masters said: 'After lunch I want you to contact Peterborough and find out at exactly what time Pamela

Parseloe reached her digs on Sunday night. Discreetly. I'll give you the address, and do it while the locals are at the inquest.'

Unconsciously Hill kept pace with Masters. Across the square and up the High Street.

'Where now, Chief?'

'The vicarage. You can do something for me.'

'What's that?'

'Chat up the elder daughter, Pamela, while I have a short word in private with Cora.'

'Will she like it?'

'She'll try to stop it.'

Hill said: 'Let her try. I can question her about that story of the headmaster's. About her father trying to get her a job in the school.'

Pamela was not pleased. She and her sister were intending to eat an early lunch before the inquest. Masters saw it laid out on the kitchen table. A faded seersucker cloth, holed in places. A segment of Dutch cheese with red plastic rind. A glass ovenware plate with half a pound of butter. A coburg on a board and four apples laid in a heap. Cora said: 'Would you like a cup of tea, Mr Masters?' Masters declined, and Hill said: 'Can I take Miss Parseloe off to another room and get the statement, sir? I'll try to be quick and not hold up their lunch.'

Masters said: 'Good idea. Make it snappy.'

Pamela demanded: 'What statement?'

Hill said: 'Sorry, I haven't explained. I'm the shorthand writer. Mr Baron gave us some information which we'd like you to confirm. So if we could step into another room, Miss . . .'

Pamela went. Unwilling and ungracious.

Masters said to Cora: 'Now, perhaps you can help me.' She folded her hands and looked at him trustingly. 'Do you remember Inspector Green coming here for the school key?'

'He said you sent him.'

'I did. He's my chief assistant. You told him the key had gone and then it came back again.'

'Yes, but he's got it now.'

'It's quite safe. Now, try to remember. Did you make the phone call to Dr Barnfelt before or after you saw the key had gone?'

She said simply: 'After it was gone. Pam said she felt the flu coming on again so would I ring and ask the doctor to come.'

'She didn't seem ill to me.'

'I didn't think she was, but she told me to say it was urgent.'

'Did the doctor give her some medicine?'

'I think he must have done. She went out just before Mr Green came. I thought she must have gone to the chemist.'

'Thank you, Miss Cora. Don't say anything about this to your sister. Keep it our secret. And now let's talk about something else. I've been talking about you to Dr Frank Barnfelt. He'd like you to visit him. Can you go this evening? About six o'clock?'

'What for?'

'Because he tells me you've never been to see him although he's your doctor. And he'd like a talk. Will you go?'

'I'd like to—if you think it will be all right.'

'I'm sure it will. Mrs Barnfelt wants to see you, too.'

Pamela, from the doorway, said: 'What's all this?'

'I was giving your sister a message from Dr and Mrs Barnfelt. They would like to see her. Miss Cora is on his list of patients, you know, though I understand she has never consulted him professionally. He thinks it would be a good thing if she were to call.'

'Does he? What if Cora doesn't want to go?'

'She's under no compulsion, of course. But just in case she'd like to—and she has already said she would—I'll have my car, with Sergeant Hill to drive it, outside the gate at five to six.' He turned to Cora. 'You can ride in style. How will that suit you?'

'I'll love it.'

Masters turned his back on Pamela and winked at Cora. He then said: 'We won't hold you up any longer. Goodbye.'

When they were outside, Hill said: 'Just for the record, she confirmed Baron's story about the job.'

'Thanks. Let's have a jar before lunch.'

*

Green, with a pint of draught Worthington in his hand, said: 'You didn't expect me to find the weapon in one morning, did you?'

Masters felt happy. Green had been nagging about the weapon for two days. Now he'd discovered for himself just how difficult that part of the problem was, and how they would have made no progress at all had they concentrated on it exclusively from the beginning. He said: 'No, I didn't.

But you've obviously covered a lot of ground in cultivating that thirst. All useful routine stuff, eh?'

Green said: 'Routine's the backbone of investigation.'

'Quite. That's why I asked you to exhaust all the possibles you could think of. No whisper of a weapon gone missing, I take it?'

'Nothing.'

'No suggestion from anybody as to what it could have been?'

'Nobody's saying a word.'

Masters said: 'Tough titty. Have another.' He was at the bar when Peter Barnfelt came fast through the door and stopped to look around. With malice aforethought, Masters said: 'I'm in the chair. Let me get you a drink, doctor.'

Barnfelt said: 'I've come to warn you . . .'

Masters turned his back on him and called along the bar to Binkhorst: 'And a whisky for the doctor, please.' He turned back to Peter. 'You were saying?'

Barnfelt looked hot and cross. A vein in his left temple was doing a belly dance. In, out. In, out. He looked at Masters with angry eyes. 'I've just had a phone call from Miss Barrett.'

Masters played it cool. 'I was hoping you had.'

'What have our private affairs to do with you?'

'Nothing. But I'm a nosey-parker by profession. And sometimes I try to make up for my shortcomings by explaining to interested parties some of the things I ferret out. You'd be surprised how often good comes of it.' He took the glasses from Binkhorst. 'Here, drink this. I hope you weren't too short with Miss Barrett?'

'I repeat, it's no business of yours.'

Masters shrugged. He didn't want a row in the bar. He would have liked to shake Barnfelt till his teeth rattled. He restrained himself from doing it—just. Instead he said: 'I promise not to interfere directly in your love-life again. Now let's talk about something else. Have you inspected the carpenter's thumb lately?'

Barnfelt stared at him as though he were mad. 'Carpenter?'

'The chap who got a chisel cut last week.'

'I don't know what you're talking about. If I did, I wouldn't answer. I've told you before, my patients' affairs are their own business—and mine. Not yours.'

'Sorry. Just trying to find common ground for a chat.' He lifted his glass. 'Cheers.' Barnfelt sulkily followed suit.

*

Spaghetti Bolognaise for lunch. Gina serving. Masters said: 'How's Maria? I saw the doctor was here earlier.'

Gina said: 'She is well. Very well. And she seems so happy. After the death of the father.'

'It seems unkind to say so, but isn't it just possible that she is feeling relieved.'

'At this murder that is done?'

'Not by the murder. By the fact that everything is now out in the open.'

Green said: 'Perhaps she's talked to the doctor about an abortion.'

Gina dropped the plate she was carrying. It clattered on the table. 'That is wicked.'

'Are you going to encourage her to keep the baby?'

'Of course. It shall not be murdered like its father.'

'Good. I'm sure you'll make a first-class grandmother.'

'It will be what I have to pay for not being a good mother.' She left the room blindly. They finished the course in silence.

After they rose from the table Green said: 'Now what? More legwork?' It was a challenge, Masters thought. A dare. So he answered: 'Yes.' Green stared in disbelief. Masters went on. 'I've given Hill the job of checking Pamela Parseloe's timings on Sunday night. I'd like you and Brant to come with me.'

They set out across the square. Rooksby was quiet. The shops closed for half day. Green said: 'Where to?'

'As far as the schoolroom.'

Green grunted. Half in pleasure at the short distance. Half in scorn. 'What the hell d'you expect to find there?'

Masters replied airily: 'I don't know. But even if it's nothing it won't be worse than your score this morning.'

'Why go? The lads have been over it with a small-tooth comb. Not a flea.'

They turned into Church Walk. Masters said: 'There's been something bothering me. I can't tell you what it is, but I'm positive it's something to do with the schoolroom. If I can just get in there and think and look . . .'

They used the front door. The back entrance had been reboarded when the sergeants had finished their inspection and the duty constable relieved.

The classroom was as they had first found it, with the exception of the corpse.

*

They'd been there two hours. Green's cigarette ends littered the floor. Brant was prowling round. Masters was sitting on a bench, feet resting on the blackboard table. The present silence had lasted nearly twenty minutes. Brant was whistling soundlessly through his front teeth. Green said suddenly: 'Face up to it. We've been all over this room a dozen times. We're getting nowhere.' He stopped in front of Masters. 'You'll never hit the nail on the head sitting here. And I could do with a cup of tea.'

Masters lowered his feet from the table and stood up slowly. He looked at Green for a moment, not seeing him. Then, absentmindedly, he said: 'Thank you.'

'Thank you? What for?'

Masters walked across to the upright plank nailed to the wall and stained with Parseloe's blood. He looked at it carefully for a time and said quietly: 'That's it. By God, that's it.'

Green was beside him. 'What is?'

'I remember now. We scoured this plank, looking for a bullet hole, didn't we?'

Green looked enquiringly at Brant and then said: 'We did. And we didn't find a single mark.'

'Exactly. But we should have done.'

'Of course we should have done. That's what the rest of us have been pointing out for days.'

Masters said: 'Don't you see? If I'd fixed that plank to the wall there would be marks. Hammer marks, all round every nail head.'

Brant was holding his breath. Green said: 'Yes. There would. If you did it. But they're professional carpenters. They don't bodge jobs like do-it-yourself amateurs.'

Masters said: 'Even when driving masonry pins into bricks and mortar? Of course there should be hammer marks—that is, if they used a hammer.'

'Meaning what?'

Masters turned from the wall. 'Think,' he said. 'What was it Dan Coulbeck said about Harry Pieters? When he put up Parseloe's shelves? "He used a bolt-setting tool on the plates".' He turned to Green. 'You called these, plates. Remember?'

Green nodded.

Brant said: 'And when Sarn't Hill and I asked Pieters for a list of his tools . . .'

Masters snapped his fingers: 'There was a bolt-setting tool among them. Right. What is a bolt-setting tool? In my ignorance, I assumed it was some sort of spanner. But it begins to look as though I was wrong. Does either of you know? No? Then we'd better find out. But before we do, just one more thing.'

He left them and walked round the room, inspecting the plates on the other three walls. He came back and reexamined the stained one. He said: 'That's it. There are nine nails in each of the other three. One every four courses. About a foot apart. There are ten here.' They counted for themselves. Brant said: 'And the one near the blood is only about seven inches from the one above and five from the one below.'

Masters nodded. 'An extra nail. And that, I think, is our projectile. Nicely hidden by being driven home in a plank of wood.'

Green let out an involuntary sigh. 'It takes some believing.'

Brant said: 'I suppose you want Harry Pieters?'

Green said: 'And his tools.'

Masters said to Brant: 'Collect the car and Hill and get Pieters. Try to be back here in half an hour. Remember Pieters will have been at the inquest, so I can't say where you'll find him.'

Brant went off at a half run. Masters sat down again. He felt momentarily weak. Green said: 'There's a transport caff on the High Street. I don't expect it shuts on early closing day.'

They went out without another word. The café was grubby. Decorated in fly-blown dark green paint. Green said to the proprietor: 'A pot for two. No. Make it for four, and strong enough for eight.' He got his way. They were obviously known. The tea was like tar. Masters drank it like nectar. The afternoon had drained him. The caffeine and tannic acid restored him. They were back in the schoolroom before the half hour was up.

Green said: 'A quarter to five.'

'I want Hill to take Cora to see Dr Frank Barnfelt in about an hour's time,' Masters said.

Green stared at him. Unable to understand. Masters knew Green couldn't appreciate how he—Masters—could think of what he—Green—considered to be an irrelevance at a time like this. It gave Masters a feeling of superiority—the sweet, better feeling of giving rather than receiving. He took out his pipe. Then sadly put it back in his breast pocket. He'd forgotten. The Warlock Flake tin was now empty, and he'd failed to pick up another from his bag at the Goblin. Green said: 'Have a Kensitas. Go on. You're on edge.' Masters wondered how Green knew. But somehow, at times like this, Green seemed to grow more perceptive: more human. Masters took the cigarette so as not to disappoint him. He felt it was no substitute for a pipe, but it kept him busy until Pieters was ushered in.

The carpenter was nervous but, Masters felt, unafraid. He was in washed-out bib overalls. Where the braces should have buttoned, he had made do with inch long wire ovals. Under the overall a fair-isle jumper. Over it an old brown suit jacket; the side pockets overfull and sagging; the breast pocket loaded with flat pencils and a steel rule. He stood just inside the door and faced Masters. By his side, Brant. Behind him, carrying a brown canvas tool bag, Hill.

Masters said: 'Come in, please.'

Pieters said: 'I don't know about that. Have I been arrested?'

It was a surly reply. Masters guessed it wasn't meant to be obstructive. More the effort of a man at a grave disadvantage trying to reassert himself.

'No. You haven't been arrested, Mr Pieters.'

'Well, I've lost enough time today through this murder lark. Half the afternoon at an inquest to answer three silly questions. Home to get changed again, and no sooner back on the job than these blokes turn up. What am I going to live on next week? Fresh air?'

Green said: 'You're in no position to complain.'

Pieters didn't like the tone. 'Oh, yes I am. And I'm doing it. Now, you'd best be quick or I'm going.'

Masters said: 'I honestly believe it will be in your best interests to help us now. If you refuse we'll have to think you've something to hide.'

Pieters walked forward. 'You're trying to soft soap me. I've nothing to hide.'

'I'm glad of that. Let's sort things out, shall we? Sit down.'

Pieters sat on the bench opposite Masters, who said: 'You fixed those timbers to the walls, I think?'

'That's right.'

'How?'

'With a bolt setter.'

'And what is a bolt setter?'

The answer came without thought. 'It's a gun.'

There was a moment's silence.

Masters said: 'A gun for firing nails?'

'That's right. Hell of a kick it needs, too, to drive pins into masonry.'

Masters said heavily: 'Mr Pieters, a man was shot dead in this room three nights ago. Didn't it occur to you that he might have been killed with your bolt setter?'

''Course not. Why should it?'

'You left it here over the weekend?'

'With all my other tools, yes.'

'And you never gave the matter a thought?'

'No. All I knew was that he'd been shot. I took it to mean somebody had used a proper gun on him—revolver or pistol or something.'

'Or something's right. I believe it was your bolt-setting tool.'

'It couldn't be. How would he know how to use it? I mean, you've got to know how to load it and . . .' Pieters stopped and looked at Masters. 'Here, you're not thinking . . .'

Masters looked back at him and said nothing. Green said: 'You know how it works. You threatened to get even with Parsloe.'

'That's as maybe.' Pieters was getting excited. 'And I wasn't the only one who had it in for him.'

'We know. But we haven't come across anybody else who owned and knew how to work a bolt setter.'

Pieters looked at Green, angry eyes. 'Haven't you? Well, you haven't looked very far. What about Perce Jonker? He sells 'em.'

Masters said: 'Who to?' Menacingly quiet.

Pieters looked down and said more slowly: 'Well, he sold me mine, and I know he's got one more in stock.' He looked up. 'Go on. You ask Perce. I'll bet you he knows how to work it.'

Masters said: 'In the dark?'

'I don't know about that. But I buy my cartridges from him, so he'll have some of them handy, too.'

Masters said: 'All right. For the moment we'll believe you didn't fire it at Parseloe. But somebody did, so let's have a look at it.'

Hill dumped the toolbag on the blackboard. Pieters got to his feet and rummaged inside. He brought out a purple tin box about ten by five by three. Masters took it from him. Opened it up. The weapon—a lumpy pistol. Lying on its side in a padded nesting compartment. Around it, in clips and grooves, spare barrel, push rod and brushes. Clipped inside the lid an instruction leaflet—virtually new. Masters took both weapon and leaflet. He took minutes over reading the instructions, and seconds over the gun. Green looked over his shoulder. The other three watched closely.

Masters said to Pieters: 'What did you use in this room? Butt-head nails?'

Pieters said: 'That's right. Two inch.' He took a small cardboard cube from the bag, opened it, and handed Masters a white metal pin. The butt head was a tenth of an inch deep, a quarter of an inch in diameter. The shank was only half as wide as the butt. Masters looked at Green and said: 'Long sharp point, long straight shank, thickening out into a wide heavy head. How does that match with the properties we suggested the projectile had?'

Green said: 'It fits exactly. What's that little red washer for? It's in a daft place.'

Near the nose of the nail, just above the chamfering, was a push fit, red plastic washer. Green went on: 'Shouldn't that be near the head?'

Masters said: 'I don't believe it is a washer in the real sense of the word. If it were, it'd have to be metal. I think it's a guide to make the shank fit the barrel—to bring it up to the same calibre as the head. Like sabot ammunition.'

Green understood. He'd fired sabot anti-tank shell in the latter years of the war. Hill didn't. He said: 'Could you explain a bit more, Chief?'

Masters said: 'The calibre of the barrel is a quarter of an inch. So's the head of the nail. So the nail will pass along the barrel quite easily. But the shank is narrower than the head, and so isn't a tight fit in the barrel. Consequently, when you press a nail in, the shank may lie a bit askew in the barrel. If you were to fire like that, the nail would come out at an angle, and lord knows where it might not go. But with the washer to act as a spacing piece—centring piece would be a better term—the shank becomes the same calibre as the head, the nail goes home sweet and true, and comes out straight.' He looked at Pieters. 'Am I right?'

Pieters said: 'That's true enough. If you want a real washer you can get a washer holder for the gun, or even some pins with metal washers already attached like those red ones. But I didn't want washers for this job. I wanted the nail heads driven right home, you see. Those red ones disintegrate on impact, mostly, an' disappear without stopping the pins going right in.'

Masters said: 'So here you used the quarter inch barrel and quarter inch cartridges?'

Pieters dipped into the bag again. This time he brought out four or five small round tins, two inches in diameter and less than an inch deep. Each had a different coloured label on the lid. He said: 'Here y'are. Green—that's weak. Yellow—where's yellow?—that's medium. Blue—strong. Red—very strong. And this black—that's superpower. It'd drive a nail through from here to Australia.'

Masters took the tins and opened them. Cartridges—slightly stubbier than two-two's, wadded and crimped. He said: 'I think we've got it all.' He picked up the gun and said: 'What's this called?' He had his finger on a plate two inches square and half an inch thick, fixed at the business end of the barrel.

'Safety shield,' said Pieters. 'You have to press that hard up against something before you can fire.'

Green said: 'To cock it, you mean?'

Pieters nodded.

Masters said: 'A hard push? How hard? Hard enough to bruise a man's chest?'

Pieters said: 'I reckon. But you'd best try it to make sure.'

Masters turned the pistol grip anti-clockwise, pulled it back, and opened the gun. He peered into the chamber. It was empty. He closed and locked it. Then he looked up at Hill and Brant.

Brant opened his jacket. 'All right. I'll buy it, Chief.'

'Over by the wall.'

It took a lot of strength to force the shield back. If Brant had not had his back to the wall, Masters thought, he'd have staggered away. But trapped as he was, his chest provided a strong enough medium. When Masters lowered the cocked gun, Brant opened his shirt. The imprint of the shield was there. Red and square, and faintly angry. Masters stopped him from refastening the buttons, and kept his eye on the mark. It gradually lost shape and diffused. Green grunted: 'Two minutes forty.'

Masters said: 'Thanks. I hope it didn't hurt.'

'Not so's you'd notice, but you used a hell of a pressure.'

'It needed it. You were like a sponge.'

Brant buttoned his shirt. Hill said: 'Well, I'll be off now. Back soon. Just taking Cora for a ride.'

Masters turned to Pieters. 'Come and look at this nail.' He led him over to the stained plank. As soon as he saw the out-of-place pin, the carpenter said: 'That's not one of mine. See? I always aim plumb for the middle of a brick. This one's hit the mortar. Look at all these others.' He started to cross the room.

Masters said: 'We've already examined them all.'

Pieters said: 'Now you've found all this out you'll be thinking more than ever that I did old Gobby in.'

Masters said quietly: 'No.'

'No?'

'We never think of a man as guilty until we've proved he is. We consider everybody, of course. And I've no doubt in my mind that the weapon used was your gun. But I'm so far from proving you guilty that when we've finished our talk you'll be able to walk out of here a free man.'

Green snorted in disbelief. Pieters stared, openmouthed. Brant whistled between his teeth. Masters went on: 'But before you go, I'd like you to do something for me.'

'Yeah?'

'Fire a nail through one of the other planks. Into a strip of mortar.'

Green burst out: 'You're not going to let him get his hands on that thing and load it, are you?'

'Why not?'

Green set his mouth and turned away. Brant moved in unobtrusively behind Pieters. The gun was loaded, cocked and fired. The spent cartridge was ejected automatically. The report in the room was shattering. Pieters said: 'And that was only a strong cartridge. Not very strong or super. I keep them for concrete.'

Masters said: 'Somebody should have heard that on Sunday night.' He stepped close to look at the nail. It was a replica of the others. He said to Pieters: 'Thanks. I'm afraid I'll have to hang on to your bolt setter.'

Pieters said: 'And when do I get it back? I've a living to earn, you know.'

Green said: 'We'll get you one on hire.'

Masters asked: 'Did you miss a cartridge on Monday?'

Pieters shook his head. 'I'd only miss one from a new box.'

Green said: 'And the murderer knew enough to pick up the spent cartridge. Very helpful.'

'It certainly shows he knew what he was doing,' Masters said.

'I always pick them up. When you go on a training course by the makers, they tell you to.'

Masters nodded. He returned the gun to its box and said to Pieters: 'When did you put these plates up?'

'Them? Let me see now. Last week sometime. Yes. Thursday it 'ud be. Thursday morning, because I had a day and a half on the ceiling joists before the weekend.'

Masters said: 'Thank you. Now, just one more job. I want that stained plank down and a two foot piece round that out-of-place nail sawing out. Without touching the nail at any time. Can you do it? It's worth a quid for a good, quick job.'

Pieters and Brant selected the tools. Masters and Green wandered out of earshot. Masters spoke quietly for a few minutes, then Green said: 'What? You want me to go to London tonight?'

'Yes please. With Brant.'

'I suppose you're right. I'd better do it myself than phone through. And there's roast lamb for dinner tonight. Gina told me.'

Masters said: 'You can go after dinner. You won't be able to do anything at that end till tomorrow morning.'

Green offered him a Kensitas. 'Except deliver your bag of spuds, I suppose.'

Masters grinned. 'I told you that would work out just fine, didn't I?'

Green sneered. 'You'll be telling me next you'd got this job buttoned up yesterday.' He didn't sound too unbelieving. Whenever the job took a turn for the better, Green couldn't help being as pleased as anybody else.

Chapter Seven

Pieters, sworn to secrecy, had gone. Hill had returned. Masters handed the two feet of planking to Green. 'Ask forensic to let me have at least a preliminary verbal report on the nail by tomorrow. If you can get through your other business by lunchtime perhaps you'll be able to bring both reports back with you in the afternoon.'

Green said: 'Should do. I'll stow this plank. We'll go straight after dinner.'

Masters thought Green was setting too much store by a bit of roast lamb. 'As you like. The roads will be clearer, later.'

Green pretended he hadn't heard. They left the school and locked up behind them. Masters said: 'I'm going to see Dr Frank Barnfelt.'

'About little Cora, I suppose.'

'I'd like to know if there's anything can be done for her. I'll be back for dinner.'

*

Dr Barnfelt saw him in the surgery after the last patient had gone. He said: 'You want news of your protégée?'

'If there is any.'

'No promises. But I think between us—medicine and welfare—we may be able to do something. To rehabilitate her is probably the best way of describing it.'

'Can you give me any details?'

'No. For two reasons. One, I don't know enough about her after only a very cursory examination, and two—you know—ethics.'

Masters grinned. 'As long as there's some chance.'

Barnfelt said seriously: 'I will do my utmost to see that what can be done for her will be done. Immediately. You have my word for it.'

Masters said: 'That's no more than I expected. But it doesn't mean I'm not grateful. I am. Very.'

Barnfelt gazed at him. Masters felt he was being analysed. Wondered what he had said that could be taken the wrong way. He could feel

Barnfelt's shrewdness. The eyes twinkling behind the pince-nez were sizing him up. Then Barnfelt said: 'How is the investigation proceeding?'

'Very well—I think. We've been here little more than forty-eight hours and we've turned up at least a dozen motives for murder. I'm afraid your vicar was a most unpopular and unsatisfactory person.'

'His reputation was not good. I am only speaking from hearsay. I had very little to do with him. Nothing socially. But doctors are recipients of confidences and news, so they know most of what is afoot—particularly in a place as small as Rooksby. One thing, however, surprises me. You mentioned motive. My knowledge of the law is limited, but I thought that to prove motive was unnecessary.'

Masters smiled. 'Limited knowledge? I've heard different.'

'Checking up on me?'

'On everybody. And you're quite right. I've no need to prove motive, but experience has taught me that ferreting out a good, juicy motive not only helps an investigation, it helps with a jury, too.'

'So you concentrate on motives?'

'And opportunity, and feasibility, and credibility, and every other thing I can think of.'

Barnfelt placed the tips of his bony fingers together. 'Does a superfluity of motives give you cause for complaint?'

'None. No complaint at all.' He grinned. 'Except one.'

'May I ask what it is?'

'As it concerns you, yes. Your two-way radio is almost on top of my frequency.'

Barnfelt looked suddenly concerned. 'But we have an allotted wavelength, and we're crystal controlled, so it is impossible for us to wander off our own frequency on to somebody else's.'

Masters said: 'I'm pulling your leg. You haven't inconvenienced us.' He noticed that Barnfelt still seemed a little concerned. He felt pleased about it. He liked causing a flutter among the apparently unflappable. He wondered what reply Barnfelt would give. When it came, it was totally unexpected.

'I must reduce power.' Barnfelt was almost talking to himself. A savant considering a problem.

Masters said: 'You mean you designed the radios yourself?'

'Yes. Yes, I did. You see, the usual V.H.F. sets are so limited in range that they are practically useless if the stations are not intervisible. So I designed an ordinary H.F. set which was small enough for our purpose, but had the traditional range.'

'Dry battery? Or do they use the car batteries?'

'Neither. I designed a power take-off from the engine, and installed in the circuit a small twelve volt Aldis lamp dag. Do you know, we can operate even if the battery is right down, so long as the engine is running? All the cells are needed for is to iron out the surges in the power supply.'

'At what range can you work?'

Barnfelt lost his eagerness. He looked down. 'Oh, several miles. I don't know exactly. It depends on conditions.'

Masters felt this was wrong. He thought a man as precise as this would know the answer to within a hundred yards. He didn't pursue the matter. He said: 'Interesting. You ought to patent it.' He stood up. 'Thank you for the news about Cora. I'll not keep you any longer.' At the door he stopped and asked: 'How did the inquest go?'

'We learned nothing new. My evidence was exactly as I gave it to you—without the suppositions, of course.'

*

Hill said: 'She couldn't have gone by train. Her landlady says she was surprised to see her before the arrival time. She also says she heard a car at the door, which didn't sound like a taxi. And the ticket collectors neither remember Pamela arriving, nor did they take a ticket from Rooksby to Peterborough at the barrier on Sunday night.' He looked across at Masters. 'Is that what you wanted, Chief?'

They were all four in Masters' room. Masters occupying the chair. Green astride the case stand. Hill and Brant perched on the bed. Masters had unearthed a new tin of Warlock Flake from his kit. The air was heavy with smoke.

'Just what I wanted. I knew Pamela Plum-Bum was lying. It'll give me great pleasure to tell her so. Now, let's see where that leaves us. She left Rooksby—we presume—at six, or a minute or two after. The landlady doesn't know to the minute when she arrived, but she puts it at ten past seven. Certainly not more than five minutes either way. Correct?'

Hill nodded.

Masters said: 'How long to get to Peterborough?'

Brant said: 'Depends on the car and the driver. But not more than three quarters, not less than half. I'd do it in that if I had to—on a Sunday night with not much traffic about.'

'We'll estimate forty minutes. That means she would arrive in Peterborough by about a quarter to seven.'

'Unless she didn't leave Rooksby till well after six,' Green said.

'I'm pretty sure she's not the type to hang around for long on a cold, windy night. So we'll assume she went off by five past.'

'Then the car must have stopped on the way. A bit of quiet snogging if all they say about parsons' daughters—and this one in particular—is true.'

'That's it. It must be. And it makes everything fit.'

'Is that the lot, then?'

'Yes. Unless anybody saw Superintendent Nicholson today.'

Hill said: 'I did. He said nothing new came out at the inquest. P or PU as expected. Funeral on Saturday. Some suffering Bishop is coming to do it.'

'Suffragan.'

Green said: 'I wonder how many mourners there'll be—genuine ones?'

Masters said: 'We'll not be among them. Now, how about a quick one before dinner?'

After Green and Brant had set out, Masters said to Hill: 'I want you to go alone to the spit and sawdust tonight.'

'Any special reason?'

'Very special. You've to act normally.'

'Is that all?'

'It's important. I don't want to change the pattern of our habits: to give anybody ideas. What you've got to do is go in there as if you were still on the lookout for snippets of information. Don't say the others have gone to London. Don't give the impression we've finished the job. And don't suggest, either, that we're not getting anywhere. People can sniff these things out like dogs smell fear. And I don't want them to suspect what stage we've reached. We've the best part of twenty-four hours to wait in suspended animation, and if the slightest whisper gets out during that time we may be caught with our trousers down. Understood?'

'If you say so. But I don't know where you've got to.'

'On purpose. That way you can't let anything out inadvertently.'

'What about Harry Pieters?'

'We've got to trust to luck there. He's promised not to talk, and I've steered clear of asking Perce Jonker any questions about bolt-setting tools so that he can't jabber around. Tomorrow's going to be tricky. So the best plan is for you and me to get out of Rooksby for an hour or two.'

'No car.'

'Ask Vanden to get you a local one. For nine o'clock in the morning. We'll take a look at the countryside.'

For Masters, the evening session in the saloon bar was a difficult one. He wanted to be up and doing. Worried by delay. Fearful it might rob him of victory. Uneasy.

He met de Hooch, Baron, Jan Wessel and Arn Beck. Was asked how he was getting on. Was non-committal in reply, and wondered whether even this evasiveness might not be open to misinterpretation. He cast around for some question to ask. One that would seem natural and relevant. He chose Parseloe's wife. She was connected—tenuously—with the case, but unlikely to evoke awkward questions for him. 'Mr Baron, did you meet Mrs Parseloe much?' He was conscious that it was a soft question. Without bite. He didn't like asking it. He wondered what he'd say if Baron said no and refused to expand.

Baron didn't. 'Too much. She got the idea that because I was the headmaster of the church school my wife should be the head cook and bottle washer for the vicar's wife. Naturally we had other ideas, but Mrs P. was a sticker. She was always on the doorstep for something or another.'

Masters leaned back. He felt the conversation would keep flowing without much help from him. He wasn't mistaken. Henry de Hooch said: 'Calling for mid-morning coffee and afternoon tea, was she? She had her rounds, you know. Twice every day she got fed in a different house. She even tried calling on us, uninvited, on afternoons when my wife was holding bridge parties. Big eats on those days. But what a mistake to make! To interrupt women at bridge!'

'I may be wrong, but I've always believed Gobby's main trouble was his wife,' Jan Wessel said. 'She depressed me, so what she did to him, living with her, lord only knows.'

'Completely unattractive,' said Baron. 'Mentally and physically. And with so many negative qualities thrown in that living with her must have been like having the invisible man about the house.'

Arn Beck said: 'The marriage was a contrived tragedy.'

'What do you mean—contrived?' de Hooch asked.

'When I had occasion to speak to the Rural Dean I was told their story. As a sort of extenuating circumstance for behaviour in Parseloe which I considered distinctly unChristian.'

'Go on,' Baron said.

'He came from quite a poor family. His parents were devoted to the church, but in a bigoted sort of way. No humour, no pleasure in religion. You must know the type. They're not as common these days as they once were, although I understand that there are some sects developing today which have much the same sort of outlook. Almost from the day of his birth his parents' great ambition was to see their son a parson. And to do him credit, he won his way through. But all three of them had distorted ideas about the clergy. Almost the only man of standing they'd ever spoken to was their own vicar. He was kind to them, and they almost worshipped him in return. To the mother and father, the idea that their son could become like this man was their individual promise from heaven. What they didn't appreciate was that their parson was a gently nurtured man, in a good living, and with a private income of his own to make it easier for him to keep up the standards they aimed at. But, even with the poorest possible start, young Parseloe reached his first goal. He was ordained. Then came the rub. Marriage. By this time all three Parseloes were lifting their sights. As a parson, the lad was accepted—as all professional men seem to be. Vocations give a social cachet. But whereas a penniless doctor or solicitor can hope to provide for a wife and family within a reasonable time, a parson may not be quite so lucky. Stipends being what they are.'

Beck stopped to drink. de Hooch called for another round. 'Where did he pick her up?' Baron asked.

Wessel said: 'She was a cut above him, I'd have said.'

'She was,' Beck replied. 'Youngest daughter of new poor. And an unattractive one. That's why she was available. He thought he was marrying into a good family. She accepted him because he was a parson. It was, as I said before, a contrived tragedy. Each thought they were getting somebody better than they could have hoped for. And that really is tragedy.'

'You mean she tried to upper-crust him from the start?' de Hooch asked.

Baron said: 'She was definitely the one who thought he ought to be the squarson. He'd have been better off with a less pretentious, more genuine woman. I can't believe he ever got any happiness from the marriage—or his kids.'

Masters put down his glass. 'It never ceases to amaze me how often murder is the sequel to a tragedy rather than the tragedy itself. This time it's the result of a mistake in the choice of marriage partners.'

Wessel said: 'And before so very long you'll have some other similar cause to investigate. I think an unrelieved diet of murder would be more than I could stomach.'

Masters entertained them with a few interesting anecdotes until Binkhorst called time. When the bars had cleared Binkhorst said: 'Have one with me, Mr Masters.' Masters accepted. He'd waited until now to break the news that Green and Brant would be away for the night. He implied that they had been called back in connection with some completely different enquiry. He made very little of it at all. The main point was that at this late hour the Binkhorsts would be unlikely to mention it to anybody outside.

*

At nine o'clock next morning, with Hill at the wheel, they left Rooksby. Masters, sitting beside him, said: 'I want to find Jeremy Pratt. We'll go to Spalding and ask at the station there.'

The police at Spalding directed them to Boston. There they found a shipping office: The Wash and Holland Line.

Masters left Hill in the car and called on Jeremy Pratt alone. He found a tall, well set-up man of thirty. A forelock of auburn hair tumbled over the forehead. The eyes were brown and frank. The face lean, the mouth smiling. Pratt was very surprised at the visit. He said: 'I'm more than pleased to meet you, Chief Inspector. But I can't help wondering why you're here. And feeling a bit queer in the stomach because of it.'

'I often have that effect on people. It passes off as soon as I assure them I'm making nothing more than a courtesy call.'

Pratt waved him to a chair. 'Courtesy call? On me? You wouldn't waste your time. But if you say so, I'll believe you. How about some coffee?'

'I could do with at least a pint of strong black if you can manage it.'

Pratt grinned. 'That reassures me.' Masters had intended it should. He loved the feeling of importance his job gave him, but he rarely wanted to inspire fear. Particularly not today. Even though he was out killing time and indulging a whimsy he had an objective in mind.

Pratt called for coffee and then sat behind his desk. He looked at Masters and said: 'I thought you'd be in Rooksby. The papers have been full of the murder and your presence there.'

'These investigations take me out and about at times. I had to come this way on another little errand, and as I had one question I thought you might answer for me, I dropped in. I hope you don't mind?'

'Not in the least. I'm genuinely pleased to meet you, but for the life of me I can't think what question I could possibly answer for you. It is almost ten years since I was in Rooksby. In fact, I've made a point of never going back.'

'Why?'

Pratt blushed. Masters thought he looked very young; and gave him full marks for having the grace to look embarrassed. Pratt said: 'You must have heard that I used to visit Rooksby a lot at one time, otherwise you wouldn't be here.'

Masters nodded.

'Then you'll have heard about Maria Binkhorst and me and how I let her down.' He sounded bitter.

Masters said: 'I understood it was your father who was the nigger in the woodpile.'

'He was—but only because I was weak and let him get away with it. And I've been too ashamed to go back to Rooksby since. But you have a question to ask.'

Masters started to fill his pipe. 'Ah, yes. Now as you can probably guess I've been checking up on the movements of practically everybody in Rooksby who was out and about on Sunday night when the vicar was killed. One of them was Binkhorst . . .'

'On a Sunday? He never used to go out on a Sunday. That was Maria's night off—or one of them.'

'Quite. That's why Binkhorst's absence from his bar interested me.'

'But you can't possibly suspect him. Why . . .'

'I suspect everybody, Mr Pratt. At least if they're sculling about on some unusual errand as Binkhorst was.'

'What was he doing?'

'Looking for Maria, he says.'

'Where?'

'That's the point. He says he went to your house near Spalding.'

Pratt looked astounded. 'Why, for heaven's sake?'

'Never mind why for the moment. He said he arrived at the gates of your house and found them padlocked. Would that be correct?'

'Absolutely.'

'Are the gates always padlocked at night?'

'All day as well. Have been since before Christmas. The house is empty. The old man died, you see.'

'And your wife didn't fancy living there?'

'My wife? Here, hang on a moment. I haven't got a wife. But I do have a bachelor flat here in Boston.'

'Sorry.' Masters didn't sound sorry. He lit his pipe. 'I should have checked on you before I came. But you can confirm that Binkhorst was right when he said the gates were padlocked?'

Pratt nodded. He was looking thoughtful. He said: 'You haven't told me about Maria. Is she married?'

'No.'

'When she was out on Sunday night, what was it? A man?'

Masters said airily: 'I suppose her father thought it was.'

'You mean he thought she was with me?'

'Yes.'

'Good heavens, why? I haven't seen Maria for ten years. Why should he think she was with me?'

'He had his reasons. Chiefly because Maria apparently hasn't encouraged many boy friends since your time.'

Pratt said: 'And I've been the same about women. I've tried, but it was never the same. Would Maria see me if I called at the Goblin, do you think?'

Masters shook his head. 'I shouldn't do that.'

'Why ever not? If she's not married?'

Masters said: 'You'd only rub salt into old wounds.'

'Do you really think so?'

'I'm certain. She's pregnant, you see.'

'Maria? Pregnant? And unmarried?'

Masters nodded.

'It takes some believing. She was always so . . . so virginal.'

'Not any more.'

Pratt walked over to the window. His back to Masters. 'Won't the chap marry her?'

'He can't.'

'I see. Married already.'

'That's not the reason. He's dead.'

Pratt swung round. 'Dead? Would I have known him?'

'I expect so. By name at any rate.'

'Who?'

'Parseloe.'

The effect on Pratt was as dramatic as Masters had intended it should be. He stood so still he scarcely breathed. At last he said: 'The murdered vicar? That old . . .' He didn't finish. Masters got to his feet. Pratt came towards him full of purpose. 'If what you've told me is true, he deserved what he got.'

Masters said: 'Maybe so. But now you know why you wouldn't be welcome in Rooksby. Goodbye, Mr Pratt. Thank you for the information and the coffee. Sorry to have been the bearer of such bad news.'

Masters saw himself out. Pratt was still standing in the middle of his office. Masters joined Hill and asked to be driven back to Rooksby. He sat silent all the way, but every so often Hill got the impression that he was smiling to himself.

*

Green and Brant arrived in Rooksby at half past three. They joined Masters and Hill in the police office. Green said: 'You're right. Blood and guts on the nail. Official report coming later.'

'And the other?'

Green nodded and handed Masters an envelope. 'It's better than even you thought it might be. It helps your case besides giving specific information.'

The thin sheaf of papers took Masters less than three minutes to read. He looked up and said: 'Give me half an hour and then ring up Nicholson and tell him to get here as quickly as possible.'

'Don't you want me with you?'

'There are one or two other things I want you to sort out. First, Pamela Parseloe. I want to know how she got to Peterborough on Sunday night. At least, I know already, but I want a statement. A true one this time, even if you've got to twist her tiny neck to wring it out of her.'

'Leave it to me. What else?'

'Pick up Peter Barnfelt and arrange for us to use private rooms at the Goblin. I don't want everybody in one office like this, all at the same time.'

'O.K. You're taking Hill?'

'And the car. But if you need it, there's a buckshee one from the local force parked near the pub. Brant had better take over the keys from Hill.'

Green said: 'I'll bring Pamela Plum-Bum in here. Then if it takes me very long to sort her out, I'll be on the spot.'

'Good idea. There is possibly one more thing we might have to prise out of her later.'

Masters and Hill left. Masters said very quietly when they reached the car: 'Dr Frank Barnfelt.'

Hill rang the house doorbell. Mrs Barnfelt answered. She said: 'My husband is just having tea, Mr Masters. It's the first time he's had a break today. Can't whatever it is wait till later?'

'I'd rather see him now, Mrs Barnfelt.'

She started to object. Barnfelt himself appeared at the door of the sitting-room down the passage. He said: 'Invite the Chief Inspector in for a cup of tea, Vera.'

Reluctantly Mrs Barnfelt opened the door wider to admit Masters and Hill. Barnfelt, table napkin in hand, ushered them into the sitting-room where a tea tray was set in front of the fire. He said: 'Sit you down. No, Vera, don't you bother. I'll get another two cups.'

Before Masters could say they wouldn't stop for tea, Barnfelt had gone, closing the door behind him. His wife said: 'Frank and Peter are really being rushed off their feet at the moment. I know your enquiry is important, but murder coming on top of a flu epidemic does make it hard work for them. All these inquests and interviews.'

Masters said: 'I quite understand. And believe me I'm very sorry to intrude on what little leisure time Dr Barnfelt has.'

'Did you come about Cora? You needn't worry about her, you know. I've never known Frank devote so much time and energy to anybody's welfare before. He's treating her as a very special case indeed.'

The door opened and Barnfelt said: 'Because she is a very special case, my dear. I feel a great responsibility towards her.' He put the cups down and turned to Masters. 'As I think you appreciate.'

Masters nodded.

Barnfelt went on: 'I'm happy to tell you that I've completed what I consider to be first-class arrangements for her. To last, I hope, for the rest of her life.'

'I'm very pleased to hear it. No, thank you, we won't stop for tea. I was about to tell you, but you went for the cups so quickly I didn't manage to get it out before you'd gone.'

Barnfelt's eyes twinkled behind his pince-nez. He said: 'I know.'

His wife said: 'You knew? Then why dash off like that?'

Masters said hurriedly: 'Just one question, doctor. Why did Maria Binkhorst come specifically to see you last week, or the week before, when her normal doctor is your son?'

Barnfelt smiled. 'She told you she came?'

'Please answer my question.'

'Then she didn't tell you.'

'You mean she didn't come?'

'No. I don't underestimate your intelligence, Chief Inspector. I should be foolish to do so when you are capable of . . . er . . . divination of so high a degree. You know why she came to me.'

'I think I can guess. She thought she was pregnant, but wished to have an older man confirm it. And probably she felt the need of an independent confidant—knowing how badly her parents would receive the news.'

Mrs Barnfelt said: 'Maria? Going to have a baby? Who's the father?'

Barnfelt said: 'You may well ask, my dear. I had to wheedle hard to get it out of her.'

'Who? Not . . .?'

'Not Peter, my dear. Parseloe.'

'Oh, no. That poor girl. With child to a man like that. And now he's dead. But I can't help feeling it's a blessing he is.'

Barnfelt said: 'Quite. I'm pleased you take that attitude, my dear. I, too, feel that Parseloe is better dead.'

Masters said: 'I'd like you to come with us, doctor.'

Mrs Barnfelt said: 'Go with you? Whatever for?'

Her husband said: 'Don't worry, my dear. Statements have to be taken officially, you know. Please get me my coat.'

She murmured: 'Yes, of course,' and hurried from the room. Barnfelt picked up his cooling cup of tea and finished it. His wife held his coat for him and handed him a muffler. He said: 'If I'm not back in time for surgery, let Peter know.'

They were in the hallway of the Goblin. Hill had escorted Barnfelt into the dining-room. Green said: 'Nicholson's on his way over. He wanted to know it all, so I told him there was nothing I could tell him over the phone except that he was to get here pronto. Right?'

'Good. And Pamela?'

'Getting anything out of her's as difficult as trying to poke smoke up a cat's backside with a knitting needle. But I managed.'

'How?'

'I murmured in her little ear that accessories to crimes are treated the same as principals. She coughed all right. Young Barnfelt did take her to Peterborough. And they stopped for a snog on the way. She says she lied to protect him, but now we've discovered for ourselves that he's the murderer she feels entitled to speak up for her own protection.'

Masters growled: 'I thought that's what she was thinking. Have you still got her?'

'In the office, with Vanden keeping an eye on her.'

'Good. I'll probably want her again. And Peter?'

Green said: 'We're having a bit of difficulty with him. He's been invited to the party, but refuses to come. Brant is tailing him, but we could have a bit of trouble persuading a busy doctor to leave his patients—without using a warrant.'

'I want him. Wessel's a magistrate and lives practically next door. Get him to sign one of the ready-use warrants.'

'What charge?'

'Accessory—for the moment.'

Green lit a Kensitas. 'We are having fun, aren't we? When's the showdown?'

'As soon as Nicholson's here. Keep Peter on ice.'

Green turned his coat collar up and left. Masters hung about near the main door. Binkhorst in carpet slippers and braces shuffled out to him with a large breakfast cup of tea. He said: 'You'll be wanting this. I made it myself, so it's a proper brew.'

Masters accepted. 'Thanks. Don't let us upset your routine. And please don't talk to your customers about what's going on, after you open.'

Binkhorst said: 'These women can smell trouble like a cow smells water. How long'll you be? Dinner an' all that.'

'A couple of hours, maybe. We'll finish as soon as I can make it, anyhow.'

Binkhorst left him. Almost immediately the front door burst open and Nicholson came in like a full back going into a tackle. 'What's up? Run into trouble?'

'No. Nothing like that. But it's your case. I thought you ought to be here to hear the facts and make the arrest.'

'Arrest? Who?'

'Dr Frank Barnfelt.'

'You can't be serious. What would he do it for?'

Masters put his cup on the hall table. 'It's to hear his reasons that you're here.'

'I'll not like arresting the doctor unless I'm sure.'

Masters said: 'He's in the dining-room. I've got Hill there ready to take shorthand. I'd like to start straight away.'

They went in. Barnfelt was sitting at the table smoking and writing on a note pad. He looked over his pince-nez as they entered, dipping his nose downward to peer at them. He said: 'Ah! Chief Inspector and Superintendent Nicholson. Is the inquisition about to start, gentlemen?'

Masters drew out a chair and sat opposite him. He said: 'Dr Barnfelt, at this point I must caution you formally. Everything said now, including this caution, will be recorded. I have reason to suspect you guilty of the murder of the Reverend Herbert Parseloe at eight o'clock or thereabouts last Sunday evening. You are not obliged to say anything . . .'

'I know. And please record that I do not wish for the presence of a solicitor.'

'You're sure?'

'Positive. I think I can trust to my own legal knowledge at this stage.'

'Very good, doctor. Do I take it that you wish to make a statement?'

'Oh, no. That is not my idea at all. I wish to hear why I'm here—why you're so sure I'm guilty.'

Nicholson said: 'That'd be most irregular.'

'Nevertheless, gentlemen, I must insist. Otherwise to keep me here you must charge me.'

Masters thought that this wouldn't please Nicholson, who'd already announced he wasn't prepared to arrest the doctor without good, solid proof. So he said to the Superintendent: 'With your permission, sir, I think in these circumstances that it would be better if I were to outline our case.'

Barnfelt looked at his watch, and then waited for Nicholson's reply.

'Whatever you think best.'

Masters turned back to Barnfelt. 'Now, doctor, I must go back several weeks, and start with Miss Parseloe. She is known to the police here as a girl who steals men from other women—openly. Making no secret of her conquests and ruining many affairs. But I have information that though she was here for the Christmas holiday and went about in Rooksby, she acted very much out of character. She had no overt affair with any man. If she was operating, it was done clandestinely.

'The leopard doesn't change its spots, doctor. So when I heard that only ten days after returning to Peterborough she came back to Rooksby with no more excuse than a mild bout of forty-eight hour flu, and stayed a fortnight to get over it, I surmised she must have—as one of the constables put it—some unfinished business to attend to. Romantic business. But again, whatever the affair, it was conducted clandestinely.

'I tried to find a broken romance—the sure sign of Miss Parseloe's depredations. Your son and Miss Barrett were no longer on speaking terms, supposedly after a few cross words over a call at bridge. I found it hard to believe that two intelligent people should carry a lovers' quarrel so far, unless there were more serious grounds. The local constables were aware of the quarrel and were able to assure me that though Miss Barrett had often been seen in the last fortnight without an escort, your son had been keeping company with an unknown girl. The only characteristic of this girl they could give me was that she had dark hair—as seen through the windscreen of a fast car.

'Most girls in Rooksby are married so early that there are very few mature enough—and still personable enough—to interest a man like your son. And yet it must have been a local girl. Had she been an outner, it is unlikely he would have been seen with her so often in Rooksby. He would have met her, and left her, presumably, near her home, because there is little to attract young lovers to Rooksby. So, a local girl, dark haired, and of a type to interest a young doctor! As far as I could make out there were two. Maria Binkhorst and Pamela Parseloe.

'I've already said I had reason to suspect that Miss Parseloe was carrying on a clandestine affair. If she could bother to come home—to her particularly unpleasant home—with a minor illness, to be treated by your son, who is not her registered doctor, it seemed likely to me that she would be the one I was interested in. But I discovered there was also some mystery surrounding Maria. More about that later.

'Doctor, I think you only tried to mislead me twice. But in fact, inadvertently it was three times. The first, and inadvertent time, was when you told me your son had been at a bridge party last Sunday evening. You honestly thought he had gone to play with Mr and Mrs de Hooch. I learned that he hadn't done so. And yet you should have known—or so I believe—because your son returned home about eight o'clock on Sunday evening. A fact you didn't appear to know. I wondered if it could have been that you were out at the time—although you assured me that you were in—on duty.'

Barnfelt spoke for the first time. He said: 'Bless my soul, did Peter actually go back to the house?'

'He did. And he appears not to have told you. I think the reason why will be apparent later.

'Now we come to the murdered man. He had an unenviable reputation; but one that he thoroughly deserved. You told me yourself that as the local doctor you gather information like a magnet attracts iron filings, and that you were well aware of Parseloe's unsavoury character. Probably you regarded him as a man mentally ill—a paranoiac or schizophrenic.'

'The former,' said Barnfelt. 'Delusions of grandeur and a persecution complex. He'd been brought up to believe that the cloth would be a magic vestment that would waft him to unprecedented heights in every walk or facet of life. He worked hard to achieve it, and then found that nowadays both the vocation and its rewards have been devalued. He'd been robbed of his dream and he'd also married a woman who brought no more to the union than an inflated opinion of her own importance and a sense of love and charity that would have disgraced a cold rice pudding. Such men are dangerous. Parseloe was a menace to this community.'

Masters said: 'You're not pulling your punches, doctor.'

'The time for that is past.'

'To go on. Maria Binkhorst found she was pregnant by Parseloe.'

Barnfelt interrupted again. 'You may think that strange. A young, lovely girl submitting to an old fiend like Parseloe. But he was as clever as Satan in some ways, you know. With a facile tongue. So many of these men become so. Superficially—after years of preaching. They learn their craft in the pulpit.'

'I understand. Maria came to you for a pregnancy test. I guess that you were so surprised to find Maria—of all people—following what appears to be the accepted course for young women in Rooksby, that you persuaded her to name the father. And that news, I suspect, angered you more than ever against Parseloe.

'By a stroke of luck, without which the best of us sometimes fails, I learned that you and your son, in your private cars, carry radios which work to each other and to a control set in the surgery. The average number of patients on a general practitioner's list these days is at least two thousand five hundred. Here, in Rooksby, there are too few inhabitants to complete one list, and yet there are two very busy doctors. This must mean that your catchment area covers not only the village, but a large area round about. Large, because it is sparsely populated and would not yield the capitation figures for two of you unless you went far afield. This led me to suppose that your wireless sets have a range of many miles.

'Now you are an able man, doctor. Both in theory and practice. You built your sets and their special power supply to fulfil the needs of a far-flung practice. You could give me all the technical information about those sets except the one fact I really wanted—their range. That was a mistake, doctor. And I knew you were dodging the issue because last Sunday evening you had your control set switched on. Why, I don't know. Probably you were tinkering, or you habitually keep it switched on—I can't tell. But I know you heard a conversation that took place somewhere along the road to Peterborough.'

Barnfelt said: 'Could I interrupt a moment, please. I am out of cigarettes and should like another packet—and a drink if possible. I see it is now half past five—the witching hour for the Goblin—and as we've been virtually sitting on the doorstep, as it were . . .'

Masters turned to Hill. 'Would you please get Dr Barnfelt a packet of . . .'

'Twenty king-size, tipped. Any sort,' said Barnfelt. 'And a large gin and tonic if that is permissible. I am not yet under arrest and so I believe I'm within my legal rights to ask for sustenance.' He smiled at Hill. A little, toothy smile. He took a well-worn wallet from his inside pocket and handed over a note. 'Can I persuade any of you gentlemen to join me?'

His offer was declined. Courteously by Masters. Somewhat brusquely by Nicholson who showed he thought this way of conducting an interview to be highly irregular.

When Hill returned he was accompanied by Green who nodded to Masters and sat down beside him.

Masters said: 'I should like to go straight ahead, doctor.'

'Please do.'

'The conversation that took place on the road to Peterborough. Between your son and Miss Parseloe. Miss Parseloe has, throughout this case, exhibited a degree of stupidity which surprised me. She told me she left her home at six o'clock on Sunday evening in the hope of thumbing a lift to the station. I refused to believe this for several reasons. First of all, she had a heavy suitcase, and under no circumstances could I envisage her running the risk of having to carry it a mile to the Halt. Which she may well have been forced to do, because it is doubtful whether many cars pass through Rooksby at that time on winter Sunday evenings. Second, her father had a car and enough time to run her to the station and be back in good time for Evensong. And third, if her father had failed her, as a girl earning her own living—an adequate one—she could and would have afforded a taxi from the local garage. So I assumed she had arranged a meeting which she didn't want me to know about. Surely an odd thing for a young girl to mislead me about during the course of an investigation into her father's murder?

'At that time I wasn't sure whom she had met, but you will remember that I saw your son paying her a visit immediately after my first interview with her. I couldn't understand this. She was perfectly well. I'd been with her for nearly an hour and I'd seen it for myself. And later you told me you had been asked to send him round urgently. From the evidence of this bogus call and for the reasons I have already outlined, I felt justified in supposing that Doctor Peter had arranged to—and, in fact, did—take her to Peterborough.

'A little later, Inspector Green was looking into the question of the keys of the school. Anybody could have broken into the hall through the makeshift barrier, but the classrooms were locked. The Inspector discovered that there were four master keys. One in possession of the builders; one with the former headmaster; one normally kept on the vestry keyboard; and one normally kept in the vicar's desk. He established that the church key was the one found on the dead body, and that the one normally kept in the vicar's desk had been missing at the time of my visit, but had reappeared before his visit. The only other caller, besides myself, at the vicarage so far that day had been your son. It seemed fair to assume that he could have returned the missing key. Called to do so by the bogus request for urgent medical attention.

'But how had Doctor Peter got hold of the key? The vicar had borrowed the church key. As I have reason to believe that he knew, before he left the vicarage that evening, he would be visiting the school after Evensong, it seemed strange that he should not take his own key, unless he intended that it should be handed to whoever was to meet him later. If Doctor Peter had it, only one person could have given it to him. Pamela. For what reason?

'Cora told us that for much of the Sunday afternoon her sister and father had been carrying on an important conversation from which she had been excluded. Important enough to need one daughter out of the way, and serious enough to prevent an avowed believer in siestas from taking his afternoon nap. What were the matters of such moment? I believe them to have been a discussion—probably started by the vicar—about his daughter's relationship with Doctor Peter. And I believe he instructed his daughter to give the school key to your son and order him to present himself at the school at eight o'clock that evening for a heart to heart talk. And I also believe I know what the talk was to be about.

'The vicar was devious minded. He chose the school for the meeting when his own study was available. He went across to the church early to avoid meeting Maria Binkhorst. I feel free to suppose that it was to avoid meeting Maria on the way back to the vicarage—at an inconvenient moment—that he decided on the school. A typical resolve of a secretive, devious mind.

'And now we come to the radio message. I checked up on Pamela's time of arrival in Peterborough and came to the conclusion that there had been a halt on the way. What happens in a car during a halt on a dark night when two youngsters of opposite sex are alone? On this occasion, probably nothing more than a kiss and a cuddle. But Doctor Peter's Triumph is cramped quarters, and I believe that some movement depressed the toggle switch of the car radio transmitter and that you, at the control set at home, were an unwitting eavesdropper on an illuminating conversation. I imagine it started amicably enough and then developed along the lines I have already indicated. Pamela Parseloe, so long unsuccessful in finding a suitable husband, intended to marry your son. Her father had pointed out how it could be done. He was to play the part of outraged father of aggrieved and wronged girl, accusing your son of unprofessional conduct. Don't forget she was technically his patient while he was in attendance on her. So Pamela was instructed to tell Doctor Peter that her father wanted to see him in the school after Evensong, and she gave him the key to let himself in if needs be. Probably Peter scented danger. I suspect he demurred. What did he say? That he was due at a bridge party at the de Hooch house? An excuse which he thought up on the spur of the moment but which you believed? Whatever it was, I suggest your son saw the pit yawning before him and struggled to get out of meeting Parseloe.

'You were listening in. You probably understood better than Peter that Parseloe meant business. You could read his mind like a book. You knew what he had done to Maria and realized that he would stick at nothing to gain his ends. And you saw the alternative facing your son more clearly than he did himself. Marriage to Pamela or a complaint that would result in his being struck off the medical register.

'You decided that neither should happen. You have been described to me as being inordinately proud of your son. Could you let him be struck off? Could you let him marry the village harlot who had probably seduced him deliberately with this end in mind? I think that was the choice you were faced with last Sunday night, doctor.'

Masters stopped for a moment. Green passed him a sheet of paper. While Barnfelt offered his cigarettes round, Masters skimmed through Pamela's statement. He then said: 'I have here Miss Parseloe's statement, made whilst we have been talking in this room. What she says substantially supports my suggestions about what happened on the journey to Peterborough and the whereabouts of the keys. Incidentally, she believes your son to be guilty of her father's murder and—reading between the lines—it looks as if she'd had hopes of using this knowledge to force him into marriage.'

He gave the statement back to Green.

'Now, to get on. As I said, I believe you realized your son's danger more readily than he did himself. You decided that as he had declared his intention of not meeting the vicar, you would keep the appointment for him. You went along to the school, on foot, and followed Parseloe into the classroom that was being divided into offices. It was not the first time you'd been there.

'Last Thursday morning a workman had cut his hand with a chisel and you had been called in to attend to it. It was just at the time Harry Pieters was using a bolt-setting tool—a masonry gun—for fixing timbers to the walls. As a practical man, a builder of locomotives and radio sets, it would be impossible for you not to be interested in this novelty. As a former medical officer of a front line regiment, well acquainted with firearms, you would be well aware of how it functioned. After watching Pieters in action for a few minutes you would be as capable of using it as he was.

'When you decided to meet Parseloe, what preparations did you make? Did you think the tools would be there in the school over the weekend, or did you play safe and prepare a syringe of, say, bismuth chloride for an intravenous injection?'

Barnfelt grinned his little grin, showing his teeth. He said: 'I told you you are not a man to be underestimated.' He looked at his watch. 'Ah, six o'clock. Time for my surgery. I hope Peter has it in hand.'

Masters gazed at him fixedly for a moment. Then went on: 'You did prepare an injection? Never mind. I can see the objections to bismuth chloride. It's lethal, and untraceable in the urine, stomach contents or blood, but it takes three or four hours to work. Had you used it, you'd have had to keep Parseloe prisoner for that time or he could have got away and told somebody.

'When you arrived at the school—it had to be after Parseloe—what did you do? Keep him talking? Listen to him while he thought you were pottering about with the workmen's tools? You were in the dark—half dark, anyway—so merely in the light from the windows he didn't really see what you were doing. He knew you as a practical man so it wouldn't surprise him, whatever you were doing, until you turned and threatened him. Forced him back, taking care to see he was carefully placed in front of one of the timbers. Then—well, we all know the rest. You cocked the gun by forcing the safety shield against his heart, and then you fired. The masonry pin went through his body and the wood, into the wall. Unfortunately, unlike Harry Pieters, you hit a fillet of mortar instead of the middle of a brick.

'After that, you collected the spent cartridge—probably using a torch for light—put away the tools—well wiped, no doubt—and left. You were careful to leave the door open—to leave the field wide open, as it were. Unfortunately, your son had come back to Rooksby and run his car on to the garage apron. I believe he went in to consult you, found you weren't there—probably thought you were out on a case—and decided he had better go to the school and placate Parseloe until such time as he could decide what to do.

'He, too, went on foot, because I suppose he didn't want his car to be seen in Church Walk. He approached the school—and here, quite frankly, I am deducing—from the back. He was late. The constable said his car entered Rooksby just after eight, so it could have been twenty past when he reached the school. As he drew close, he saw a figure leaving the building, rather stealthily I should imagine. Peter must have drawn back in the shadows to remain unseen—in case it was Parseloe. But he recognized it as you as you passed. I should think it was at that moment that he remembered he had found his transmitter switched on, and realized what you could have overheard. That is why he didn't speak to you. Instead, when you had gone, he went into the school. He found Parseloe. There was nothing he could do for him, so he withdrew, and for some unknown reason, used the key Pamela had given him to lock the door behind him. I think it was a reflex action. An effort to lock away, out of sight, the proof of his father's deed. But whatever it was, it left us to find a locked door, with the dead man's key still in his pocket. And that helped.' He turned to Green. 'That was why I had to ask you to make a special point of key chasing. It was important.

'When Pamela came back to Rooksby, she believed Peter had killed her father. It was a natural supposition, but I don't believe she cared a scrap, beyond wanting that key back. Hence her urgent call for medical attention.'

Masters pulled out his pipe and began to fill it.

'Now you, doctor, as I said, tried to mislead me twice. You were very helpful over the wound. Being an intelligent man you obviously realized that it would be wiser to appear helpful, because I could get the same information elsewhere if needs be. But you really did make a mistake when you suggested that the bruise had been made by a prod with the end of a piece of squared timber. I put it down as the suggestion of somebody who had not seen the wound, and as an impossible suggestion from a knowledgeable physician who had made a thorough inspection and taken measurements.

'The second time you tried to mislead me was when, by refusing to tell me what was wrong with Maria, you tried to suggest there was some quite serious ailment. In fact, it was plain to see that the girl was blooming—literally. And even my limited knowledge of such things includes the fact that when she is expecting a baby a girl may suffer headache, flatulence and dyspepsia at night, and sickness in the morning. I wondered why you had tried to pull the wool over my eyes—because in order to attempt it you must have known the true story—and decided that you could have learned it from your son that morning or, equally likely, you could have known of it before your son.'

Masters struck a match to light his dead pipe. 'That's the summary of my efforts these last three or four days, doctor. I haven't yet had your son's confirmatory statement, but he will be held as an accessory until he makes it. After that, the warrant will be squashed.'

'If I make a statement later—and this is a promise you can record—can my son go to attend to our patients? You can always get him back again if necessary.'

'I appreciate your concern for your son and your patients. The efforts you made on Cora's behalf—to get the arrangements completed before this meeting could happen—also weigh with me. With Superintendent Nicholson's permission your son can be allowed to take surgery.'

Nicholson agreed reluctantly, and Green left to tell Peter Barnfelt he was free, temporarily. Masters turned to Frank Barnfelt and said: 'To support my case, doctor, I sent Inspector Green to London with the masonry pin for scrutiny. The report is that it still has traces of blood on it. Also, I asked him to consult our archivist to discover whether there are any previous deaths known to have been caused by masonry guns. There is one. The account was written up by the doctor who was called in. It was an accident. In an office building. The joiner concerned misjudged the thickness of an internal wall. It was too thin. The pin went through it and passed through the body of a man working in the next office. He died. The report appeared some years ago in The Aesculapian. The journal's publishing office has told us that at that time you were on its screening panel, and were one of three doctors who read the article for medical accuracy before publication. So probably the idea was not entirely new to you.'

Barnfelt said: 'You're a very thorough man, Chief Inspector.' He glanced down at his watch. 'Nearly a quarter to seven. How time flies. Do you think I could have another drink?'

Green returned to report that Peter had gone. 'He's still bolshie. Won't play.'

'Wouldn't you be bolshie to a policeman investigating a murder you know your father has committed?' Masters turned to Barnfelt. 'I'm sorry to say that his attitude did help to convince me that he had some guilty secret. Not that I blame him. It was quite a load to bear.'

'Thank you. Peter hasn't mentioned it to me, so I didn't know until you told me that he even suspected me. I feel sure he won't think too badly of me when he has had time to consider matters.'

Nicholson got to his feet. He said to Masters: 'Can I have a word with you in the hall?'

They passed Hill as he brought in Barnfelt's drink. Masters said: 'What's the matter? Isn't the case open and shut enough for you?'

Nicholson said: 'Of course it bloody well is. God knows how you've done it in the time. Three days! It'd have taken me three months. Who'd ever have thought of a masonry gun? I'd never even heard of one. I'm grateful, see. Very grateful. But I hate the thought of charging a police surgeon. Can't your Inspector do it?'

'It's your case.'

'I know, but I still don't like it.'

Masters said: 'Then don't charge him.'

'What?'

'My personal belief is that you won't get a chance. I'm almost certain he's been too clever for us.'

'How d'you mean?'

'Well, I thought that if a doctor wanted to commit suicide he'd take an overdose of one of the fast acting barbiturates. He'd be dead within an hour. Barnfelt didn't die within an hour, and showed no symptoms of distress, so I thought we were all right. But did you see him when I mentioned intravenous bismuth chloride? And notice how often he looked at his watch?'

Nicholson said: 'Here, come on. We'll have a look at him.' He made for the dining-room door.

Masters held him back. 'Steady. If he did administer it, it's too late.'

'How d'you know?'

'The only time he has been alone was when we called at his house and he went to the kitchen to get more cups. If he took it, it was then. At four o'clock. Probably the syringe he prepared for Parseloe. A quick jab into the ante-cubital vein in the forearm. Done in no time. It works in three to four hours, and it's seven o'clock now.'

'And symptoms?'

Masters shook his head. 'No pain. They just flake out, suddenly.'

They stood silent for a moment. Masters said: 'Don't look so miserable. If it's happened, it's nobody's fault.'

'Why should he do it? He'd not even been questioned.'

'He knew. I've tried to keep things secret, but I had to ask about those wireless sets. There would be no reason for my doing so unless I was pretty sure of myself. And besides, he knew that by injecting himself he couldn't be accused of suicide, or of murder.'

'How come?'

'You can't say a man's a murderer until he's been tried and found guilty. And you can't say he's committed suicide if you can't trace the bismuth chloride—and you can't. He's protected his family all right.'

'Always supposing he's done it.'

'Always supposing. But he must have done. Otherwise he wouldn't have been so occupied with the way the time was going. And, of course, he wouldn't have offered to make a statement later. He knew we wouldn't get it. So nobody will be able to state categorically that he murdered Parseloe. He's a crafty one.'

Nicholson said: 'And I had qualms about charging him. Come on. I'm going in. We'll get him over to the station before it happens.'

They entered the dining-room. Nicholson said to Barnfelt: 'I want to see your forearms.'

Barnfelt smiled at Masters. 'So you did know. I was beginning to wonder.' He stood up to remove his jacket. The effort appeared to be too much for him. Masters helped him down into the chair again. He looked up, showed his teeth in a little smile, and said: 'Thank you.'

Masters was wondering whether this was thanks for helping him to sit, or for allowing him to die, uncharged, with no incriminating statement made. He could come to no sure conclusion. Nicholson said to Green: 'Ring for an ambulance. It'll be too late, but get it. And his son. Son first.'

But Barnfelt died before Peter arrived. Masters said: 'Cause of death? Cardiac arrest?'

Peter Barnfelt glowered at him for a moment, and then said: 'Is that what you suggest?'

'You're the doctor. But I feel sure that whoever you get to give a second opinion will agree.'

'You won't . . .'

'Interfere? No. My report will, of course, contain all I know, but it will be highly classified. As for my team—don't worry. Why don't you ask Miss Barrett over to keep your mother company?'

*

To avoid the bars, the body was taken through the back way and out of the Goblin. Green went to release Pamela Parseloe. Nicholson to report to his H.Q. Hill and Brant to deal with the cars and type up the notes.

Masters, weary, wandered into the saloon bar. It was still too early for the regulars. He stood at the counter and asked for gin. Maria was serving. She said quietly: 'Will you be going home now?'

'Tomorrow morning.'

He thought she was looking splendid. She seemed inclined to want to stay and talk. He didn't mind. He let her prattle on without really listening. He was enjoying the wholesome look of her. That smooth lower lip that looked so inviting. Suddenly she stopped in mid-sentence. He gazed at her. Her face had lit up. Where it had been lovely before, now it was radiant with animation. He turned to see what she was staring at. Standing just inside the door was Jeremy Pratt.

Masters murmured: 'I'll leave you to it,' and moved over to the fire.